旅遊英文 這樣就GO

許惠姍　審訂

三民英語編輯小組　彙編

附電子朗讀音檔

📢 行前準備到突發狀況，各種旅遊情境都在這！

看字彙出外景，掌握旅遊英文的關鍵。

聽不懂情境對話，你需要旅遊狀況句。

運用不同句子搭配，教你還能這樣說。

現在才知道有這麼多旅遊必備小知識。

🔶 三民書局

審者序

「讀萬卷書，行萬里路。」
我總是用這句話提醒學生，在認真讀書準備未來的同時，也要找出空閒時間四處走走看看，開拓眼界、創造回憶。

讀書與旅行是生活中不可或缺的精神糧食，除了透過書本內的知識豐富人生之外，實際走出去認識這個世界能給我們寬廣的視野與體驗。當書中的歷史建築或雄偉地勢就在眼前，原本的文字及圖片彷彿躍出了小小的紙張世界，說著它們的故事，領著旅行者回顧過去的一切，這是一種無法言喻的感動、一種親身經歷的激動。更甚者，如果可以將所學的知識應用在欣賞旅行中的萬物上，那就是旅行兼學習的最高境界了。

本書提供關於旅行之行前資訊，書中按照情境介紹旅行中實用的字彙、片語及對話，也有與各情境相關的額外資訊，有了這些基礎知識，我們能安心地出國感受不同國家的風土民情與品嘗各國當地特色美食，自在地體驗旅行所帶來的樂趣與意義。

面對瞬息萬變的世界，旅遊英文不僅提供英文知識，也期盼激發對於學習新知的動機與興趣。透過不斷地接觸全球最新訊息，我們要將所學、所見、所聞整合起來，內化成自己的知識，再進一步地去認識這個世界，深度感受旅行當下的充實與滿足。

許惠姍

使用說明

1

行前準備超助攻，旅遊新手也能懂

標記相關單字，對照學習好省力！

行前準備 1
辦理護照、簽證

▼ 首次申辦護照 ▼

☆ 需要準備（年滿十四歲或未滿十四歲已請領身分證）：
1. 已經填妥資料的普通護照申請書一份。
2. 身分證正本及正、反面影本各一份。（十八歲以下者須備父或母或監護人之身分證正本及正、反面影本各一份。）
3. 最近六個月內的白底彩色照片兩張。
4. 規費。

* 首次申請普通護照者必須本人親自至外交部領事事務局或外交部中、南、東部或雲嘉南辦事處辦理。如果不能親自前往，則須先至任一戶政事務所填妥普通護照申請書並作人別確認後，再委託代理人（旅行業者或親屬）向外交部代為申請護照。

（！）護照也可

相關單字： 🎧 #1-1

❶ passport *n.* [C] 護照	❽ tourist/travel visa *n.* [C] 旅遊簽證
❷ ID card (= identity card) *n.* [C] 身分證	❾ business visa *n.* [C] 商務簽證
❸ valid *adj.* 有效的	❿ work visa *n.* [C] 工作簽證
❹ expire *vi.* 到期	⓫ student visa *n.* [C] 學生簽證
❺ renew *vt.* 換新，更新	⓬ working holiday visa *n.* [C] 度假打工簽證
❻ validity *n.* [U] 效期	⓭ visa on arrival *n.* [C] 落地簽證
❼ visa *n.* [C] 簽證	⓮ visa-free *adj.* 免簽證的

美食當前篇

餐廳預約

字彙出外景 🎧 14-1

① breakfast/brunch/lunch/dinner reservation
　　 n. [C] 早餐／早午餐／午餐／晚餐訂位
② take/accept a reservation *phr.* 接受訂位
③ hold a reservation for sth
　　 phr. 保留…(時間) 的訂位
④ modify/postpone a reservation
　　 phr. 修改／延後訂位
⑤ reservation code *n.* [C] 預約代號
⑥ party *n.* [C] 一群人
⑦ table for sth *phr.* …(人數) 的位子
⑧ be fully booked (up) *phr.* 被訂滿

⑨ non-smoking section *n.* [C] 禁菸區
⑩ parking lot *n.* [C] 停車場
⑪ parking space *n.* [C] 停車位
⑫ dine *vi.* 用餐
⑬ come by *phr.* 到訪，造訪
⑭ dress code *n.* [C] 服裝規定
⑮ dining time limit *n.* [C] 用餐時間限制
⑯ minimum charge *n.* [C] 最低消費
⑰ service charge *n.* [C] 服務費
⑱ corkage fee *n.* [C] 開瓶費

93

各種旅遊主題都給你，跟著字彙出外景

小耳機編號就是音檔號碼，跟著專業外籍錄音員一起邊聽邊說邊學，超有效率！

追追旅遊狀況句，學習各種情境對話

提供各種情境對話，遇到什麼狀況都不怕，還有中英對照好方便！

旅遊狀況句 🎧 25-5

There is a long line at the ticket office, and Jean and Hank are waiting in line for tickets.

Jean: Oh, my goodness! Look at the crowd! We have to stand in line for at least half an hour to get the tickets.
Hank: You bet! It's boiling hot. I will go and buy some cold drinks.
Jean: Get me a Coke, thanks.
Hank: OK. I'll be right back. Make sure nobody cuts in line.
Jean: No problem.

售票處大排長龍，而珍和漢克正在排隊買票。
珍：喔，我的天呀！看看這人群！我們要排至少半小時才買得到票。
漢克：沒錯！天氣好熱。我去買一些冷飲。
珍：幫我買一瓶可樂，謝謝。
漢克：好的。我馬上回來。確保沒人插隊。
珍：沒問題。

❗ 排隊時若要禮讓別人優先，請說「After you.」而不是「You go first.」喔！因為「You go first.」帶有命令的口吻，反而是不恰當的用法喔！

⬆ 你的即時小幫手，隨時補充不出糗！

4

知道還能這樣說，
　　應答自如 Follow Me

還能這樣說

1. Please give me a table in the non-smoking section.

> a table in the smoking section 吸菸區的位子
> a table by the window 靠窗的位子
> a table with a view 有景觀的位子
> a table on the balcony 觀景臺上的位子
> a table away from the kitchen 遠離廚房的位子
> a private dining room 私人用餐包廂

2. I'm sorry there aren't any tables left for 7:30 p.m.

> all the tables are reserved until 8:30 p.m. 八點半才有空位
> we don't take reservations for lunch/dinner 我們午餐／晚餐不接受預訂
> we don't take reservations on weekends 我們週末不接受預訂
> we are fully booked up/have no tables available 我們已經客滿了

色塊內文字可視情況替換，怎麼說都沒問題！

現在才知道這麼讚的知識

5

現在才知道

如何安全抵達目的地？ 🔍

在國外旅遊一定要留意自身安全，否則很容易成為不法分子下手的目標。此外，在國外自駕，除了語言不通導致不易辨識路牌外，不熟悉路況也很容易導致意外。
以下幾招報你知，讓你平平安安地出遊：

1. 善用 Google 地圖等導航網站，事先規劃路線並記錄沿途會經過的路標。如此一來，在前往旅遊地點時，也不會手忙腳亂，找不到方向。
2. 問路要問對人，熟記基本的問路用語並詢問住宿的飯店人員會是比較好的選擇；若是在路途中迷路，也盡量去附近明亮的商店內問路。
3. 即便不知道路，也不要太慌張。如果手上拿著地圖或手機，一臉慌張地找路，就很容易成為歹徒下手的目標。當有太過熱情的路人要為你指路時，也請記得保持適當距離，以免身上的貴重物品被不安好心的人扒走喔！

最實用的旅遊必備知識，讓你輕鬆成為旅遊達人，走到哪都不怕！

電子朗讀音檔下載

請先輸入網址或掃描 QR code 進入「三民・東大音檔網」
https://elearning.sanmin.com.tw/Voice/

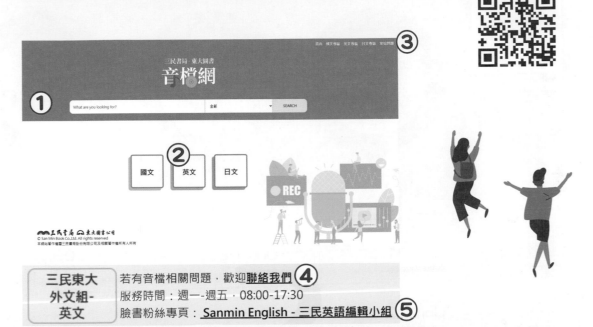

三民東大 外文組- 英文	若有音檔相關問題，歡迎**聯絡我們** ④ 服務時間：週一~週五，08:00-17:30 臉書粉絲專頁：**Sanmin English - 三民英語編輯小組** ⑤

① 輸入本書書名即可找到音檔。請再依提示下載音檔。

② 也可點擊「英文」進入英文專區查找音檔後下載。

③ 若無法順利下載音檔，可至「常見問題」查看相關問題。

④ 若有音檔相關問題，請點擊「聯絡我們」，將盡快為你處理。

⑤ 更多英文新知都在臉書粉絲專頁。

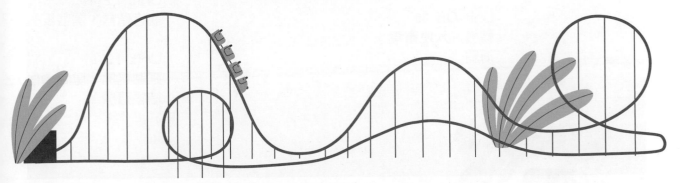

CONTENTS

行前
準備

出境
入境篇

飛航
旅途篇

安心
住宿篇

美**食**當前篇

購**物**專家篇

四**通**八達篇

突**發**狀況篇

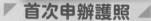

行前準備 1
辦理護照、簽證

▶ **首次申辦護照** ◀

☆ 需要準備（年滿十四歲或未滿十四歲已請領身分證）：

1. 已經填妥資料的普通護照申請書一份。

2. 身分證正本及正、反面影本各一份。（十八歲以下者須備父或母或監護人之身分證正本及正、反面影本各一份。）

3. 最近六個月內的白底彩色照片兩張。

4. 規費。

＊ 首次申請普通護照者必須本人親自至外交部領事事務局或外交部中、南、東部或雲嘉南辦事處辦理。如果不能親自前往，則須先至任一戶政事務所填妥普通護照申請書並作人別確認後，再委託代理人（旅行業者或親屬）向外交部代為申請護照。

 護照也可以請旅行社代辦喔！代辦費用依各家旅行社公告為主。

▶ **申換護照** ◀

☆ 需要申換的情形：

1. 現有護照的有效時間已到期，應該要申請換新護照。

2. 現有護照汙損以致不能使用，應該要申請換發新護照。

＊ 依照國際慣例，大部分國家或地區皆規定入境之外國旅客所持護照效期須在「六個月以上」。因此如果發現護照效期不足，要記得及早更換喔！

☆ 需要準備：

1. 已經填妥資料的普通護照申請書一份。

2. 身分證正本及正、反面影本各一份。（十八歲以下者須備父或母或監護人之身分證正本及正、反面影本各一份。）

3. 最近六個月內的白底彩色照片兩張。　　4. 繳交尚有效期之舊護照。　　5. 規費。

▶ **遺失補發** ◀

☆ 需要準備：

1. 身分證正本及正、反面影本各一份。（十八歲以下者須備父或母或監護人之身分證正本及正、反面影本各一份。）

2. 最近六個月內的白底彩色照片兩張。

3. 國內遺失：國內護照遺失申報表正本。

　　國外遺失：入國證明書及中華民國臺灣地區入出境許可證。

 更多關於申辦護照及申請簽證資訊，可至外交部領事事務局網站查詢。
一切資訊依外交部領事事務局公告為主。

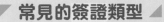

常見的簽證類型

 簽證就是一國之入境許可喔！

1. 旅遊簽證：出國目的為旅遊觀光時申請，通常允許持證人在境內停留十五到九十天。因為是持旅遊簽證，因此禁止在當地從事工作。

2. 商務簽證：用於從事短期商務活動，例如：商務洽談、表演等，屬性和旅遊簽證類似，但停留當地期間可能獲取報酬。

3. 工作簽證：允許持證人在當地從事工作，工作簽證的效期通常較長。

4. 學生簽證：供持證人在當地接受教育使用，學生簽證的效期比較長，讓持證人可以滯留到畢業。但是否允許持證人在當地打工，各國規定不一。

5. 度假打工簽證：允許持證人在旅行期間為賺取旅遊資金在當地受僱工作，效期通常為一年。

6. 落地簽證：申請人抵達目的國機場時再辦理。相較於透過駐外機構，落地簽證所需的時間較短、通過率較高。（雖然落地簽證很方便，不用事先辦理。但機場人潮很難預料，若剛好遇到大批隊伍，就只能慢慢等待。另外，若不符合簽證辦理的規定，當地的簽證官有權力拒絕給簽證，因此出國前一定要查明相關規定喔！）

▶ 各國簽證的相關規定有時會隨著國際情勢有所變化，因此出國前都要記得上外交部網站再次確認喔！

▶ 你知道臺灣人去許多國家是免簽證的嗎？快查查你的目的地需不需要簽證吧！

▶ 護照就像是在國外用的身分證，而簽證就像是外國發給你的入場券喔！

相關單字：　　　　　　　　　　　　　　　　🎧#1-1

❶ passport *n.* [C] 護照

❷ ID card (= identity card) *n.* [C] 身分證

❸ valid *adj.* 有效的

❹ expire *vi.* 到期

❺ renew *vt.* 換新，更新

❻ validity *n.* [U] 效期

❼ visa *n.* [C] 簽證

❽ tourist/travel visa *n.* [C] 旅遊簽證

❾ business visa *n.* [C] 商務簽證

❿ work visa *n.* [C] 工作簽證

⓫ student visa *n.* [C] 學生簽證

⓬ working holiday visa *n.* [C] 度假打工簽證

⓭ visa on arrival *n.* [C] 落地簽證

⓮ visa-free *adj.* 免簽證的

行前準備 2
跟團旅行、自助旅行

	跟團旅行	自助旅行
	跟團旅行就是先付款、後消費的旅遊方式，由旅行社安排規劃一切行程。通常費用全包的旅行團費用包含交通（含遊覽車、機票費用）、餐飲、住宿、觀光景點的門票等；而導遊、司機以及領隊的小費另計。	自助旅行是指不依賴旅行社，自行安排食、住、行、樂的旅遊方式，自助旅行不單指背包客或一個人獨自旅行，也可以和幾個朋友或家人共遊。 青年旅社和廉價航空常是自助旅行者的首選！
優點	1. 包吃包住，不用煩惱行程。帶上行囊就能輕鬆出發。 2. 有領隊、導遊專業服務和解說。 3. 搭乘遊覽車，交通更方便。	1. 自由度超高，日期、行程、路線都可以隨心所欲、自由自在。 2. 將預算用在真正喜歡的地方。 3. 深入探訪在地人文風情。
缺點	1. 時間、行程沒有彈性。 2. 可能會被安插購物行程。 3. 比較無法深入體驗在地生活。	1. 需要時間和精力事前準備資料（例如：入境／出境規定、當地習俗）。 2. 安全要靠自己把關。 3. 凡事都要自立自強。

小心「低價／零團費旅行團」！
選擇旅行社行程要貨比三家，了解市場行情很重要。若看到團費遠遠低於市場行情的旅遊行程，千萬要三思、不要衝動下訂。因為那很可能是旅行社藉由低價或零團費來吸引消費者報名參加，等實際出遊時再帶團員至特定的土特產店消費以賺取回扣彌補旅費。有些導遊甚至會強迫團員購物。因此千萬要留心這類低價或零團費的旅行團行程。

▼ 其他類型的旅行 ◣

1. 半自助旅行：介於跟團和自助旅行之間，部分旅遊行程由旅行社代辦，剩下的由旅行者自行安排。一般可向旅行社購買「機＋酒」行程、樂園門票或車票等。至於當地的交通、飲食和景點等就由旅行者自己規劃。

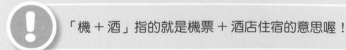
「機＋酒」指的就是機票＋酒店住宿的意思喔！

2. 戶外教育：即為學校旅行，是學校課程的一部分。學校師生走出教室外，藉由實際的感官體驗達到自我成長、社會互動、環境關係等教育目的。

3. 商務旅行：又稱為出差，除了和一般旅行一樣
   需要規劃交通、住宿、飲食外，商務旅行也會涉及宴會、會議等商務行
   程安排。而商務旅行期間的食宿費用通常由公司支付。
4. 迷你旅行：結合跟團旅行和自助旅行的優點。由旅行社為旅行者客製化出遊行程；
   參團者通常是親戚朋友，人數介於二到八人。

 迷你旅行的費用雖然比較高，但既可以玩得自由愜意，又不用煩惱繁瑣
的行程和人生地不熟的問題，是近年來盛行的旅遊方式。

▼ 旅遊保險 ◢

旅遊保險通常指旅遊不便險和旅遊平安險。當旅遊期間發生意外導致行程延宕、財產受到
損失或人體、生命受到損害時，被保險人可以申請理賠。保險期間通常即為旅行期間。

1. 旅遊不便險：主要保障旅行期間因為突發狀況而產生的財務損失。常見的突發狀況有行
   李延誤、行李遺失、行李被盜或損壞，以及航班延誤或被取消等。
2. 旅遊平安險：主要保障旅行期間個人身體、健康安全為主。因遭受意外等事故，以致身
   體受傷、失能或死亡，可獲得補償理賠以減輕醫療等財務負擔。

 許多保險公司都有推出「旅平 + 不便險」這類旅遊綜合保險，而且還可直接
在線上投保，相當方便。各家保險的條款不盡相同，因此選購前一定要仔細比
較，選出最適合自己的方案！另外若不幸遇到意外，也要記得索取相關證明文
件以利後續申請保險賠償。

相關單字： 🎧 #2-1

❶ package tour *n.* [C] 跟團旅行

❷ travel agency *n.* [C] 旅行社

❸ all-inclusive *adj.* (費用) 全包的

❹ airfare *n.* [C] 機票費用

❺ accommodations *n.* (*pl.*) 住宿

❻ tourist attraction *n.* [C] 觀光景點

❼ tour guide *n.* [C] 導遊

❽ tour leader/manager *n.* [C] 領隊

❾ independent/individual travel

   n. [U] 自助旅行

❿ backpacker *n.* [C] 背包客

⓫ youth hostel *n.* [C] 青年旅社

⓬ budget airline/low-cost carrier (LCC)

   n. [C] 廉價航空

⓭ entry/exit requirement

   n. [C] 入境／出境規定

⓮ local custom *n.* [C] 當地習俗

⓯ semi-independent travel

   n. [U] 半自助旅行

⓰ outdoor education *n.* [U] 戶外教育

⓱ school trip/tour *n.* [C] 學校旅行

⓲ business trip/travel *n.* [U] 商務旅行

⓳ mini tour *n.* [C] 迷你旅行

⓴ travel insurance *n.* [U] 旅遊保險

行前準備 3
打包行李

▶ 託運行李要注意 ◀

☆ 重量篇

1. 赴美旅客免費託運行李限額為每人兩件，每件限重二十三公斤。除往返美國外，往其他國家地區則是頭等艙及商務艙限重三十公斤、經濟艙限重二十公斤。

2. 單件託運行李一般限重三十二公斤，若超過則須分裝行李。此舉是要避免行李搬運人員受職業傷害。(限重三十二公斤亦列於部分國家的職業安全法中，例如：澳洲、紐西蘭、南非、斯里蘭卡、阿拉伯聯合大公國及英國等。)

 各航空公司託運規定不同，詳細資訊依各航空公司為主。

☆ 物品篇

1. 行動電源、備用鋰電池、打火機不能託運，須放置手提行李中。
   若為內含鋰電池的 3C 產品，例如：手機、手提電腦等，請關機後再託運。

2. 重要或貴重物品，例如：鑰匙、現金、金銀珠寶、有效證券、易碎物品等，最好不要放託運行李。因為行李可能遺失、損壞或延遲送達。

3. 寵物運送：各國及各航空公司規定不同，若要攜帶毛小孩一同出國，一定要事先查好相關規定！關於各項檢疫規定，可至行政院農業委員會動植物防疫檢疫局網站查詢。

 至香港轉機或入境香港，不能攜帶電槍類物品(例如：電擊棒)，以免觸犯當地法令。

手提行李打包要注意

1. 超過一百毫升的液狀、膏狀或帶有液體的食品（例如：布丁、味噌等）、罐頭、凝膠、噴霧劑禁止放在手提行李裡，都必須託運。
   (1) 手提行李內所攜帶之液體、膠狀及噴霧類物品之容器，其體積不可超過一百毫升，並須置於容量一公升內的透明塑膠袋中。
   (2) 嬰兒食品及藥物、糖尿病或其他醫療所需之液體、膠狀及噴霧類物品，應先向航空公司洽詢。通過安檢線時，也須向安全檢查人員申報，獲得同意後，便可攜帶上機。
   (3) 防狼噴霧劑須託運。（港澳航班則不可攜帶。）
2. 搭乘赴美航班時，除了經過航空公司檢查確認非屬危險或危安物品的藥粉、嬰兒配方奶粉及人類骨灰之外，其他超過或等於三百五十毫升之粉狀物，例如：即溶咖啡、高蛋白乳清等，都不可以攜帶上飛機。
3. 棍棒類物品都不可放在手提行李帶上飛機。
   (1) 長傘必須託運，而摺疊傘可以攜帶上機。
   (2) 攝影腳架、自拍棒都須託運。（雖然部分攝影腳架、自拍棒符合臺灣民航局規定，但可能不符合外國規定，因此建議還是託運比較保險。）
4. 運動器材，例如：棒球棍、高爾夫球杆、冰鞋等都須託運，因其具有傷害性。
5. 刀具，例如剪刀、美工刀、修眉刀等都須託運。（少部分圓頭刀具可置於手提行李，但建議還是託運比較保險。）
6. 臺灣機場出境時，可隨身攜帶一個傳統打火機上機（藍焰防風打火機不可攜帶及託運）。如果前往中國轉機或入境，則禁止攜帶任何打火機。
7. 殺蟲劑須託運；防蚊液也有可能不被允許攜帶上機，因此建議託運。

 行李的相關安檢規定隨著國際情勢時有變化，出國前可以上出境機場、交通部民用航空局及各航空公司網站確認最新資料喔！

相關單字： #3-1

❶ checked baggage *n.* [U] 託運行李
❷ free baggage allowance *n.* [U] 免費託運行李限額
❸ piece *n.* [C] (一) 件
❹ maximum weight *n.* [U] 限重，最大重量
❺ lithium battery *n.* [C] 鋰電池
❻ carry-on baggage *n.* [U] 手提行李
❼ liquid *n.* [C][U] 液體
❽ gel *n.* [C][U] 凝膠
❾ spray/aerosol *n.* [C] 噴霧劑
❿ medical needs *n.* (*pl.*) 醫療所需
⓫ approval *n.* [U] 同意，批准

出境入境篇

預訂機票

 字彙出外景

🎧 01-1

❶ airline *n.* [C] 航空公司

❷ airways *n.* (*pl.*) 航空公司

❸ airline/plane/flight reservation

　　n. [C] 機票預訂

❹ book *vi.*; *vt.* 預訂

❺ prefer *vt.* 偏好

❻ economy class

　　n. [U] 經濟艙；*adv.* 乘坐經濟艙地

❼ economy-class *adj.* 經濟艙的

❽ business class

　　n. [U] 商務艙；*adv.* 乘坐商務艙地

❾ business-class *adj.* 商務艙的

❿ first class

　　n. [U] 頭等艙；*adv.* 乘坐頭等艙地

⓫ first-class *adj.* 頭等艙的

⓬ available *adj.* 可獲得的

⓭ fare *n.* [C] 票價

⓮ e-ticket *n.* [C] 電子機票

⓯ depart *vi.* 起飛

⓰ transfer *vi.* 轉乘

⓱ destination *n.* [C] 目的地

⓲ upgrade *vt.* 使(機位)升等

旅遊狀況句

01-2

Tina is calling Panda Airlines to make a flight reservation.

Agent: Hello, Panda Airlines. May I help you?

Tina: Yes, I'd like to book a one-way ticket to Macao.

Agent: When would you like to fly?

Tina: November 13th.

Agent: OK. Would you prefer a morning flight or an afternoon flight? We have two flights to Macao on that day, one at 8:30 a.m. and the other at 2:00 p.m.

Tina: The afternoon flight, please.

Agent: One moment, please. (*After a while*) How would you like to fly—economy, business, or first class?

Tina: Economy class is fine.

蒂娜正在打電話給熊貓航空訂機票。

櫃員：你好，熊貓航空。有什麼我能幫你的嗎？

蒂娜：有的，我想要訂一張去澳門的單程票。

櫃員：你要什麼時候出發？

蒂娜：十一月十三日。

櫃員：好的。你偏好搭上午還是下午的班機？我們那天有兩個航班去澳門，一班是上午八點三十分，另一班是下午兩點。

蒂娜：請幫我訂下午的班機。

櫃員：請稍等。(*過了一會兒*) 請問你要搭乘經濟艙、商務艙或是頭等艙？

蒂娜：經濟艙就好。

01-3

Frank is calling Lion Airways to make a flight reservation.

Frank: Hello, I'm calling to book a flight to Vienna. I'd like to fly on the evening of January 5th.

Agent: We have a flight on the 5th, and it departs at 8:00 p.m. There are only business-class seats available.

Frank: What's the fare?

Agent: It's NT$45,689, including tax. Is that all right with you?

Frank: It's fine.

Agent: I'll hold a seat for you.

Frank: Can you try and find me a window seat?

Agent: No problem.

法蘭克正在打電話給獅子航空訂機票。

法蘭克：你好，我打電話來是想訂去維也納的機票。我想要在一月五日晚上出發。

櫃員：五號那天我們有一個晚上八點起飛的班機。目前只有商務艙的位子。

法蘭克：票價是多少？

櫃員：含稅價格為新臺幣 45,689 元。你覺得可以嗎？

法蘭克：可以。

櫃員：我會為你保留一個座位。

法蘭克：可以試著幫我找個靠窗的座位嗎？

櫃員：沒問題。

還能這樣說

1. I'd like to book a one-way ticket to Macao.

a round-trip ticket 來回票	Seoul, Korea 首爾，南韓
a return ticket 回程票	Tokyo, Japan 東京，日本
a nonstop flight 直達班機	Okinawa, Japan 沖繩，日本
a direct flight 直飛班機	Bali, Indonesia 峇里島，印尼
a connecting flight 轉機班機	Bangkok, Thailand 曼谷，泰國
a red-eye flight 紅眼班機	Munich, Germany 慕尼黑，德國
a 9 a.m. flight 上午九點鐘班機	Vancouver, Canada 溫哥華，加拿大
the first/earliest flight 最早的班機	Los Angeles, the United States 洛杉磯，美國

2. What's the fare?

the one-way fare 單程票價

the round-trip fare 來回票價

the fare from Taipei to London 臺北到倫敦的票價

3. Can you try and find me a window seat?

an aisle seat 靠走道的座位

a middle seat 中間的座位

a seat with more legroom 伸腿空間較大的座位

現在才知道

電子機票怎麼看 🔍

電子機票 (e-ticket) 就是機票的電子訂位紀錄，於購票手續完成後寄到訂票者的電子信箱，用以通知班機行程、班次和時間等訊息。但電子機票「不是」登機證 (boarding pass) 喔！訂票者需要依照各航空公司的規定於登機前至線上或機場辦理登機手續後，才會取得登機證。

電子機票通常有以下內容：

✈ **AIRLINES**

Electronic Ticket Receipt
① Booking Reference: XXXXXX
② Passenger　　　　　　　③ Ticket Number
WANG, HSIAO-MING　　　　　123-1234-123456

Itinerary

From ④	To ⑤	Flight ⑥	Class ⑦	Date ⑧	Departure ⑨	Arrival ⑩
TAIPEI – TAOYUAN INTL Terminal 1	TOKYO – NARITA Terminal 2	XX123	Y	02 Dec	12:50	16:50
TOKYO – NARITA Terminal 2	TAIPEI – TAOYUAN INTL Terminal 1	XX456	Y	07 Dec	15:15	18:30

Receipt

② Name	WANG, HSIAO-MING	
③ Ticket Number	123-1234-123456	
⑪ Form of Payment		
⑫ Fare		
⑬ Taxes		
⑭ Total Amount		
⑮ Issuing Airline and Date		
⑯ Endorsements		

 儘管各航空公司的電子機票有不同格式，但只要掌握關鍵字，就能找到需要的資訊囉！

① 訂位代號：有時列為 Booking Number。

② 乘客的英文姓名：有時列為 Name 或 Passenger Name，內容務必要和護照的名字一致。若不小心填錯，可能需要支付手續費修改或重新購買機票喔！

③ 機票號碼：簡稱「票號」，可以說是機票的身分證。由 3+10 碼數字組成，前三碼為出票航空公司的數字代碼，例如：中華航空為 297、長榮航空為 695、日本航空為 131、美國航空為 001。

④ 航班出發地：有時列為 Departure Airport。若機場有分不同航廈則會另外註明，例如：Terminal 1 (T1) 為第一航廈。

⑤ 航班目的地：有時列為 Arrival Airport。

⑥ 班機號碼：由 2 碼英文 +3 碼數字組成，前兩碼為航空公司代碼，例如：中華航空為 CI、長榮航空為 BR、日本航空為 JL、美國航空為 AA。一般固定航班後面再加三碼數字，如 BR607、CI983。加班機或包機則是由四碼數字組成。

⑦ 艙等：各航空公司可能有不同的列法。頭等艙的代號為 F、P 或 R；商務艙的代號為 C 或 J；經濟艙的代號為 Y、B 或 K。

⑧ 航班起飛日期：由 2 碼日期與 3 碼英文月份組成，例如：02 Dec (十二月二日)。

⑨ 出發時間：有時列為 Depart Time。多採用二十四小時制。

⑩ 抵達時間：有時列為 Arrival Time。若時間後面標註「+1」即表示加一天，指抵達時間為當地的時間。

⑪ 付款方式：標示乘客購買機票時的付款方式。

⑫ 原始票價：表示未含其他稅費的原始票價。

⑬ 稅額：包含燃油附加費、兵險附加費、機場服務費等；燃油附加費及兵險附加費依各航空公司規定計算，機場服務費因各地機場條件不同而有不同的名稱和金額。

⑭ 總票價：表示含稅後的總票價。

⑮ 發行此票的航空公司及日期

⑯ 使用限制：有時列為 Restriction。內容可能為 Non-Endorsable (不可轉讓他人)、Non-Refundable (不可退票)、Non-Reroutable (不可更改行程)，或 For... Carrier Only (限定搭乘某航空公司)。

辦理登機、
機場報到、
機票劃位

字彙出外景

🎧 02-1

❶ domestic/international terminal

　n. [C] 國內／國際線航廈

❷ check in phr. (機場) 辦理報到手續

❸ check-in (counter) n. [C] (機場) 報到櫃臺

❹ check-in agent

　n. [C] (機場) 報到櫃臺服務人員

❺ departure hall n. [C] 出境大廳

❻ seating preference n. [C] 座位偏好

❼ bulkhead seat

　n. [C] 隔間座 (飛機分隔牆的第一排座位)

❽ (emergency) exit-row/exit seat

　n. [C] (緊急) 出口座位

❾ cabin n. [C] (飛機) 座艙

❿ board vi. 登 (機)

⓫ boarding time n. [U] 登機時間

⓬ boarding pass n. [C] 登機證

⓭ boarding gate n. [C] 登機門

⓮ delay vt. 使延誤

⓯ proceed vi. (朝特定方向) 前進

⓰ terminal n. [C] 航廈

⓱ ID document scanner n. [C] 證件掃描器

⓲ security checkpoint/control

　n. [C] 安檢站／線

02-2

Mr. Jones is talking with a check-in agent.

Mr. Jones: Good evening. Is this the right counter to check in for Flight BA349 to London?

Agent: Yes. May I see your passport, please?

Mr. Jones: Sure. Here you are.

Agent: Do you have a seating preference?

Mr. Jones: I'd like a window seat near the front of the cabin, if possible.

Agent: Alright. We still have a window seat in the front.

Mr. Jones: Great!

Agent: Here are your passport and boarding pass. Your seat is 4A. The boarding time will be at 9:05 p.m. Please board at Gate 19. Be sure to arrive at the boarding gate at least 30 minutes before your flight.

瓊斯先生正在和機場報到櫃臺服務人員談話。

瓊斯先生：晚安。請問飛往倫敦的 BA349 航班是在這個櫃臺辦理登機手續嗎？

櫃員：是的。可以看一下你的護照嗎？

瓊斯先生：當然。在這裡。

櫃員：請問你有座位偏好嗎？

瓊斯先生：如果可以的話，我想坐在座艙前面靠窗的座位。

櫃員：好的。座艙前面還有一個靠窗的位子。

瓊斯先生：太好了！

櫃員：這是你的護照和登機證。你的座位是 4A。登機時間是晚上九點五分。請在十九號登機門登機。務必至少在你的航班起飛前三十分鐘抵達登機門。

 02-3

Chloe is talking with a check-in agent.

Chloe: Good afternoon. Is this where I can check in for Flight CI608 to Hong Kong?

Agent: Yes, but I'm afraid that your flight will be delayed for two hours. It will leave at 4:35 p.m.

Chloe: That's terrible.

Agent: I'm sorry, ma'am. The delay is due to air traffic control. We can hardly do anything about it.

Chloe: Alright.

Agent: I need your passport. Do you have a visa to enter Hong Kong?

Chloe: Yes. Here you are.

Agent: It's good to go. Have a nice flight!

克蘿伊正在和機場報到櫃臺服務人員談話。

克蘿伊：午安。我可以在這裡辦理去香港 CI608 航班的登機手續嗎？

櫃員：可以，但恐怕你的班機會延誤兩個小時。要下午四點三十五分才起飛。

克蘿伊：糟透了。

櫃員：很抱歉，女士。延誤的原因是航空交通管制。我們也無能為力。

克蘿伊：好吧。

櫃員：我需要你的護照。你有香港簽證嗎？

克蘿伊：有的。在這裡。

櫃員：辦好了。祝你旅途愉快！

還能這樣說

1. May I see your passport, please?

visa 簽證	credit card 信用卡
ID card 身分證	e-ticket 電子機票
Mainland Travel Permit for Taiwan Residents 臺灣居民來往大陸通行證	

> ▶ 〈行前準備 1〉提到護照就像是在國外用的身分證,那為什麼有時還可能要出示身分證呢?原來是因為當護照有汙損或標示不清時,身分證就可以派上用場證明自己的身分啦!
>
> ▶ 若在航空公司的網站購買機票,辦理登機時可能會被要求出示購買機票的信用卡,此舉是為了防範盜刷喔!
>
> ▶ 臺灣居民來往大陸通行證就是俗稱的「臺胞證」。

2. I'm afraid that your flight will be delayed for two hours.

postponed 延後　canceled 取消　rescheduled to 4:00 p.m. 改到下午四點

3. The delay is due to air traffic control.

strikes 罷工	waiting for crew 等待機組員
bird strikes 鳥擊	weather conditions 氣候因素
catering 餐飲準備	mechanical problems 機械問題
security clearance 飛安檢查	

waiting for connecting passengers/bags 等待轉機乘客／行李

knock-on effect resulting from a delayed aircraft
其他延誤航班造成的連鎖反應

現在才知道

報到登機的常見方式
（相關報到規定以航空公司說明為主。）

☆ 機場自助報到 **(self check-in)**

乘客到機場並找到自助報到機後

❶ 放入護照掃描資料或輸入電子機票
編號，以檢索航班資料。

❷ 選擇座位。

❸ 列印登機證。

❹ 前往指定行李託運櫃臺登記寄存行
李。若無需託運行李，可跳至下一
步驟。

❺ 前往辦理出境手續。

 機場自助報到讓你避開櫃臺排隊人龍，快速搞定報到手續！

☆ 機場報到登機 **(check-in)**

1. 報到手續通常於起飛二到三小時前
開放辦理，最晚須於起飛前一小時
到達機場並辦理。若太晚辦理，櫃
臺有權拒絕為乘客辦理，且損失與
責任由乘客自行承擔。

2. 乘客應事先確認自己的護照是否仍
在有效期之內，以及是否取得目的
地入境簽證。

 依照國際慣例，護照效期建議在「六個月以上」喔！

☆ 網路預辦登機 **(online check-in)**

1. 事先在網路上辦理登機，可以省去在機場排隊等候的麻煩。各家航空公司開放
   網路預辦登機的時間不盡相同。例如：中華航空、長榮航空、國泰航空為起飛
   前一個半到四十八小時。

2. 網路上辦理登機時，需填寫訂位代號、姓名 (英文)、護照資料等資訊。乘客可
   以檢視、選擇、更改或升等座位，也可以新增行李。待辦理好後，記得要列印
   出登機證或將其下載到智慧型手機裡。

    若同行者有同一組訂位記錄，那就可以一起辦理預辦登機喔！

3. 於網路上預辦登機後，若有行李要託運，乘客仍需在飛機起飛前一到二小時到
   各航空公司的櫃臺或使用自助行李託運機託運。

   若沒有要託運行李，便只要依據規定在時限前抵達登機門就可以了。

    各航空公司通常會有專門辦理託運行李的櫃臺供預辦登機的乘客使用，所以
   不必和現場辦理登機報到的乘客一起排隊，更節省時間喔！

* 若因故無法按時搭機，要記得取消已辦理的登機手續喔。

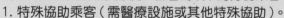

 網路預辦登機雖然很方便，但若為以下身分的乘客可能無法網路預辦登機喔！
1. 特殊協助乘客（需醫療設施或其他特殊協助）。
2. 十二歲以下單獨旅行的兒童。
3. 與嬰兒同行的乘客。
4. 團體乘客或單筆訂位紀錄人數十人及以上者。
5. 訂位紀錄尚未完成開票或機位尚未確認者。

出境入境篇

Unit **03**

行李託運、
隨身行李、
領取行李、
遺失行李

字彙出外景

🎧 03-1

❶ suitcase *n.* [C] 行李箱

❷ baggage *n.* [U] 行李

❸ scale *n.* [C] 磅秤

❹ overweight *adj.* 超重的

❺ oversized *adj.* 過大的

❻ fee *n.* [C] (*usu. pl.*) 費用

❼ misdirect *vt.* 將⋯送錯地方

❽ excess baggage *n.* [U] 超重行李

❾ lost/damaged/delayed baggage

　n. [U] 行李遺失／受損／延誤

❿ claim *vt.* 要求 (合法權利)

⓫ damages *n.* (*pl.*) 賠償金

⓬ compensation *n.* [U] 賠償 (金)

⓭ fill in/out *phr.* 填寫

⓮ conveyor (belt) *n.* [C] (行李) 傳送帶

⓯ X-ray inspection *n.* [C] X 光機檢查

⓰ baggage claim area *n.* [C] 行李提領處

⓱ baggage cart/trolley *n.* [C] 行李推車

⓲ baggage carousel *n.* [C] 行李轉盤

⓳ baggage claim information

　n. [U] 行李資訊看板

🎧 03-2

Kevin is talking with a check-in agent.

Agent: Are you checking any bags?

Kevin: Yes, this suitcase, please. I'll keep the other one as a carry-on.

Agent: I'm afraid your baggage is too big to fit in the overhead compartment. You have to check it, too.

Kevin: Alright.

Agent: Could you put them on the scale, please?

凱文正在和機場報到櫃臺的服務人員談話。

櫃員：你要託運行李嗎？

凱文：是的，請託運這個行李箱。另一個我要當手提行李。

櫃員：恐怕你的行李太大而無法放進座位上方的行李置物箱。你也得把它託運。

凱文：好吧。

櫃員：可否請你將它們放在磅秤上呢？

🎧 03-3

Viola is talking with a check-in agent.

Agent: Your baggage is overweight by 5 kilos. You'll have to pay excess baggage fees.

Viola: How much will that be?

Agent: That will be NT$1,650.

Viola: Fine. Here you are.

薇奧拉正在和機場報到櫃臺的服務人員談話。

櫃員：你的行李超重 5 公斤。你得支付超重行李的費用。

薇奧拉：要付多少錢？

櫃員：新臺幣 1,650 元。

薇奧拉：好的。錢在這兒。

🎧 03-4

Warner is seeking compensation for his damaged baggage at the baggage service counter.

Agent: May I help you?

Warner: Yes. My baggage is badly damaged. One of the wheels is broken. Can I claim damages?

Agent: Sure. Please fill out this form. The airline will take care of it.

Warner: Will they pay me compensation or repair the wheel?

Agent: The airline will be responsible for the cost of repairing the wheel. If the baggage is damaged beyond repair, they will pay you compensation or send you a new one.

華納正在行李服務臺要求賠償他損壞的行李。

櫃員：有什麼是我可以幫你的嗎？

華納：有的。我的行李箱嚴重損壞了。其中一個輪子壞了。我可以要求賠償嗎？

櫃員：當然。請填寫這張表格。航空公司會處理。

華納：他們會付我賠償金還是修理輪子？

櫃員：航空公司會負責修理費。如果行李箱損壞得無法修理，他們會付你賠償金或是寄送一個新的給你。

🎧 03-5

Cara is talking with a baggage service counter agent.

Cara: Hi, I can't find my baggage.

Agent: Please show me the baggage claim ticket and fill in this form.

Cara: How long will it take to find my baggage?

Agent: Sorry, I'm not sure. Sometimes it takes just a few hours, but it may also take a couple of days.

卡拉正在和一位行李服務臺的人員談話。

卡拉：嗨，我找不到我的行李。

櫃員：請出示行李領取票根並填寫這張表格。

卡拉：找到我的行李需要多久時間？

櫃員：很抱歉，我不確定。有時候只要幾個小時，但也有可能需要幾天。

還能這樣說

1. Your baggage is too big to fit in the overhead compartment.

within the weight limit 沒超重
overweight by 5 kilos/5 kilos over the weight limit 超重 5 公斤

2. My baggage is badly damaged.

is lost 不見了
hasn't come out 還沒出來
seems to be missing 似乎不見了
is misdirected to another airport 被錯送到另一個機場

☆ 託運行李

當乘客至機場報到櫃臺辦理託運行李時，服務人員會在行李的把手固定一張行李領取標籤 (baggage claim tag) 並將標籤尾端的行李領取票根 (baggage claim ticket) 撕下交給乘客。標籤上記載該次飛行的航班資料，例如：乘客的身分、航班號碼和目的地機場等。

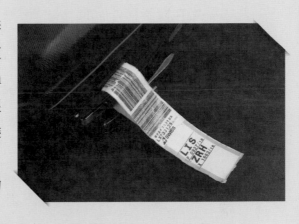

 有些乘客為了紀念，會在行李箱上留下舊的行李標籤貼紙，但這其實有可能造成條碼辨讀錯誤，進而無法使行李正確順利送到目的地。

☆ 行李遺失怎麼辦？

千萬不要放棄，如果不是惡意盜取的話，行李找回的機會很大。通常航空公司會主動與乘客保持聯繫；如果沒有，乘客也可主動向他們查詢。

1. 立即申報遺失：

一旦找不到自己的行李，就要立即前往機場行李服務臺申報遺失。

2. 妥善保存行李領取票根：

每件託運行李都有行李領取票根，通常會連同登機證一起交給乘客，記得一定要保管好。行李遺失或被誤拿，行李領取票根就是最好的憑證。

3. 保持冷靜，提供正確訊息：

提供行李箱的顏色和外形等相關資訊，並告知航班號碼。

❗ 在託運行李時，將行李領取標籤上的條碼和行李一起拍張照，若行李不幸弄丟了，可供協尋人員更快找到你的行李喔！

4. 詳細描述行李箱的內容物：

航空公司通常會詢問行李裡有什麼，描述得越仔細越能證明行李是你的。

❗ 建議出發前先列一張行李清單，不但可照著收拾行李，一旦行李遺失，也可方便又詳細地說出行李中的物品。

☆ 小技巧

1. 加上個人特色，錯拿 OUT！

   行李箱的形狀、顏色大多大同小異，若要避免自己或是其他旅客拿錯，最好的辦法就是在行李箱外面加上獨特裝飾，例如：貼上顯眼的貼紙、掛上有特色的行李吊牌或是穿上鮮豔的行李保護套等。

2. 行李箱毀損怎麼辦？

   拿到行李後不要急著拉走，記得檢查外觀，若有損毀，應立即申報。事後申報可能會因無法證明行李是於託運過程損壞，而不予賠償。

3. 行李延遲、毀損或遺失，可以索取賠償。

   行李沒有完好的跟在自己身邊，難免有些掃興。雖然各家航空公司規定不同，但只要當下向服務人員提出申告，備妥相關文件，就可以得到一定的賠償。

 若出國前有加買旅遊不便險，那就可以依保險合約向保險公司索賠。

出境入境篇

安全檢查、
登機廣播、
班機誤點、
錯過班機

字彙出外景

🎧 04-1

❶ security officer *n.* [C] 安檢人員

❷ baggage inspection *n.* [C] 行李檢查

❸ metal detector gate *n.* [C] 金屬探測門

❹ pre-boarding announcement

　　n. [C] 登機前廣播

❺ final boarding call/announcement

　　n. [C] 最後登機廣播

❻ passenger *n.* [C] 乘客

❼ inform *vt.* 通知，告知

❽ inconvenience *n.* [U] 不便

❾ air/jet bridge *n.* [C] 空橋

❿ gate agent *n.* [C] 登機門驗票員

⓫ connecting flight *n.* [C] 轉機班機

⓬ alternate flight *n.* [C] 替代班機

⓭ assistance *n.* [U] 協助

⓮ reschedule *vt.* 重新安排…的時間

⓯ update *vt.* 為…提供最新資訊

⓰ flight information board

　　n. [C] 航班資訊看板

⓱ on time schedule *phr.* (航班) 準時 (起飛)

⓲ behind schedule *phr.* (航班) 延後 (起飛)

04-2

Murray is talking with a security officer.

Officer: Please lay your bag on the conveyor belt and put your laptop and small objects in the bins. Then, step through the metal detector gate.

(*Beeping*)

Murray: What's wrong?

Officer: Please step to the side. Do you have any keys or cellphone in your pockets?

Murray: No, but I have some coins.

Officer: Put your coins in this bin and walk through the metal detector again, please.

Murray: Alright.

Officer: You're all set. Have a nice flight!

莫瑞正在和一位安檢人員談話。

安檢人員：請把你的包包放在傳送帶上，把手提電腦和小物件放在容器裡。然後走過金屬探測門。

(*嗶嗶嗶*)

莫瑞：怎麼了？

安檢人員：請到旁邊。你口袋裡有鑰匙或手機嗎？

莫瑞：沒有，但有一些硬幣。

安檢人員：把你的硬幣放在這個容器裡，請再重新通過金屬探測器。

莫瑞：好的。

安檢人員：可以了。祝你航程愉快！

04-3

Good morning, passengers. This is a pre-boarding announcement for Flight BR701 to New York City. We are now inviting passengers with small children and passengers requiring special assistance to board. Please have your boarding pass and identification ready. Regular boarding will begin in approximately ten minutes. Thank you.

各位乘客早安。這是飛往紐約市的 BR701 航班的登機前廣播。我們現在邀請有小孩或需要特殊協助的乘客登機。請準備好你的登機證和證件。一般登機將約於十分鐘後開始。謝謝。

04-4

Ladies and gentlemen, may I have your attention, please? We regret to inform you that due to the thunderstorm in Tokyo, Leopard Airlines Flight LE983 to Taipei has been delayed and is now rescheduled for departure at 3:30 p.m. from Gate C7. We are sorry for the inconvenience.

各位女士、先生們，請注意。我們很遺憾通知你由於東京雷雨的緣故，花豹航空飛往臺北的 LE983 航班已被延誤，現在將改到下午三點三十分於登機門 C7 起飛。我們對所造成的不便深感抱歉。

04-5

Daisy is asking for help because she has just missed her connecting flight.

Daisy: My flight arrived late, so I missed my connecting flight.

Agent: Don't worry. We can help you find an alternate flight. Would you show me your ticket, please?

Daisy: Sure.

Agent: I am sorry we don't have any flights leaving today. But we have one flight leaving at 9:00 a.m. tomorrow.

Daisy: OK, I will take that flight, then. But where will I stay tonight?

Agent: You may stay at a local hotel, and we will cover the cost since the flight delay is our fault.

因為剛錯過轉機班機，黛西正在尋求協助。

黛西：我的航班延誤，所以我錯過了轉機班機。

服務臺人員：別擔心。我們可以幫你找到替代班機。能麻煩你出示機票嗎？

黛西：沒問題。

服務臺人員：很抱歉，我們今天沒有任何班機了。但我們有一個明天早上九點出發的班機。

黛西：好的，那我就搭那班。但我今晚要住在哪裡？

服務臺人員：你可以在本地旅館留宿，我們會支付費用，因為班機延誤是我們的過失。

還能這樣說

1. We are now inviting passengers with small children and passengers requiring special assistance to board.

first-class passengers 頭等艙乘客
business-class passengers 商務艙乘客

2. Leopard Airlines Flight LE983 to Taipei has been delayed.

is boarding 正在登機
has been canceled 取消了
has been called for boarding 已廣播登機

現在才知道
免稅商品好划算 🔍

出國旅遊總是離不開購物，除了在目的地購物以外，機場內和各家航空公司的機上免稅商品更是不容錯過。免稅加上不定期的優惠，有時甚至比百貨公司週年慶還要划算，真的會讓人一個不小心就買到失心瘋。

☆ 機場免稅商店 **(duty-free shop)**

從國際精品到具當地特色的伴手禮，機場免稅商店應有盡有。而世界各地的機場免稅商店也有各自的價格優勢，因此建議旅客在出發前可先上網查詢。此外購物時，記得要出示護照及登機證喔。

☆ 機上免稅商品購物 **(in-flight duty-free shopping)**

除了機場免稅商店，國際航班上也是購物的好地方。很多國際航班會提供機上免稅商品的銷售服務。航空公司會和各大品牌合作，取得獨家的機上優惠價，有些甚至比機場免稅商店更划算。有機會不妨翻閱座位前放置的機上購物型錄 (in-flight shopping magazine/catalog)，看看有什麼便宜好撿吧！

❗ 不管是在機場免稅商店購物或使用機上免稅商品購物的服務，若搭配線上預購，就不用擔心現場沒貨而且優惠通常多更多喔！

出境入境篇｜安全檢查、登機廣播、班機誤點、錯過班機

	機場免稅商店	機上免稅商品購物
價格	因為免除稅金，所以價格通常較本國購買便宜。	1. 部分商品為獨家機上優惠價。 2. 有些航空公司提供哩程積分 (mileage point) 折抵消費金額的服務。
商品種類	商品種類多元、豐富。	因為飛機上的空間有限，所以品項、數量較少。
付款方式	可用當地貨幣、美金、歐元、信用卡或簽帳金融卡付款。	可用當地貨幣或信用卡付款。 (部分航空公司有限制刷卡金額。)
常見用語	1. May I see your passport and boarding pass? 我能看你的護照和登機證嗎？ 2. Sign here, please. 請在此處簽名。 3. We provide shipping all over the world. 我們提供全球遞送服務。 4. Do you want me to wrap it? 需要我為你包裝嗎？ 5. Could you wrap them separately? 請問你能將它們分開包裝嗎？ 6. How long would it take for my package to be delivered? 我的包裹需要多久時間才會寄達？	1. Have you seen our in-flight shopping catalog? 你有看過我們的機上購物型錄嗎？ 2. Would you like to order any duty-free goods? 你想要訂購免稅商品嗎？ 3. All major credit cards are accepted, but purchases must not exceed \$5,000. 所有信用卡皆可使用，但不可超過 5,000 美元的額度。 4. Please wait when I collect your duty-free goods. 請稍後，我來幫你準備免稅商品。

出境入境篇

轉機、
入境審查、
海關

字彙出外景

🎧 05-1

❶ domestic *adj.* 國內的

❷ international *adj.* 國際的

❸ layover/stopover

　　n. [C] (在飛行途中) 短暫停留

❹ transit visa *n.* [C] 過境簽證

❺ transit/transfer desk/counter

　　n. [C] 轉機服務臺

❻ direction sign *n.* [C] 指示標誌

❼ immigration (control) *n.* [U] 入境檢查

❽ arrival/landing card *n.* [C] 入境卡

❾ sightseeing *n.* [U] 觀光

❿ customs *n.* (*pl.*) 海關

⓫ customs officer *n.* [C] 海關人員

⓬ customs clearance *n.* [U] 海關通關

⓭ customs procedure *n.* [C] 海關手續

⓮ customs declaration form

　　n. [C] 海關申報表

⓯ detector dog *n.* [C] 檢疫犬

⓰ declare *vt.* 申報

⓱ prohibit *vt.* 禁止

⓲ entry *n.* [U] 入境，進入

⓳ confiscate *vt.* 沒收，充公

05-2

Noah is talking with a transit desk agent at the transit desk.

Noah: I'm to transfer to the connecting flight to Sydney. Can you help me?

Agent: Yes. May I see your passport?

Noah: Sure. Here it is.

Agent: OK. Here is your boarding pass. Your next flight will depart at Gate 6 in 40 minutes. You can directly go to the boarding gate by following the direction signs.

諾亞正在轉機服務臺和一位轉機服務臺人員談話。

諾亞：我要轉搭去雪梨的轉機航班。你可以幫我嗎？

服務臺人員：好的。可以看一下你的護照嗎？

諾亞：當然可以。在這裡。

服務臺人員：好了。這是你的登機證。你下一個航班將在四十分鐘後於六號登機門起飛。你可以循指示標誌直接前往登機門。

05-3

Stanley is talking with an immigration officer to pass through immigration.

Officer: Is this your first time in the United States?

Stanley: Yes, this is my first visit.

Officer: What's the purpose of your visit?

Stanley: I'm here for sightseeing.

Officer: Are you traveling alone?

Stanley: No, I'm traveling with my girlfriend.

Officer: I see. How long will you be staying?

Stanley: For a month.

Officer: Where will you be staying?

Stanley: We'll be staying at a youth hostel.

Officer: OK, here is your passport. You are free to go through. Welcome to the United States.

史丹利正在和一位移民官談話以通過入境檢查。

移民官：這是你第一次來美國嗎？

史丹利：是的，這是我第一次到訪。

移民官：你的入境目的是什麼？

史丹利：我來這裡觀光。

移民官：你是自己一個人旅行嗎？

史丹利：不是，我和我女友一起旅行。

移民官：了解。你們會待多久？

史丹利：一個月。

移民官：你們會住在哪裡？

史丹利：我們會住在青年旅館。

移民官：好了，這是你的護照。你可以通關了。歡迎來到美國。

 05-4

Cathy is talking with a customs officer.

Officer: Would you mind if I check your baggage?

Cathy: No problem. (*Opening her baggage*)

Officer: Is this laptop a gift for someone?

Cathy: No, it's for my personal use.

Officer: All right. Do you have anything to declare?

Cathy: I'm carrying a bottle of wine. Do I need to declare that?

Officer: No, that won't be necessary. But I'm afraid you can't bring in these apples. Fresh agricultural products are prohibited entry. I have to confiscate them.

凱西正在和一位海關人員談話。

海關人員：你介意我查看你的行李嗎？

凱西：沒問題。(打開她的行李)

海關人員：這個手提電腦是送人的禮物嗎？

凱西：不是，這是我自己要用的。

海關人員：好的。你有任何東西要申報嗎？

凱西：我帶了一瓶酒。我需要申報嗎？

海關人員：不需要。但是恐怕你不能帶這些蘋果入境。新鮮農產品禁止入境。
我得沒收它們。

還能這樣說

1. I'm to transfer to the connecting flight to Sydney.

> a transit passenger for Flight ZA306 是 ZA306 航班的轉機乘客
> connecting with Flight ZA306 要轉搭 ZA306 航班
> continuing on to Sydney 要繼續前往雪梨

2. I'm here for sightseeing.

> study 讀書
> business 經商
> visiting a friend 拜訪朋友
> attending a meeting 參加會議

現在才知道

轉機不暈頭轉向 🔍

不搭直達班機，選擇轉機班機的原因很多種，最常見的原因有減輕荷包負擔或沒有直達目的地的航班。而有些乘客也會趁著轉機的空檔來趟城市旅遊。你知道嗎？為了推廣觀光，有些機場還提供轉機旅遊 (transit tour) 的服務呢！但轉機班機也有缺點，例如：轉機時間較長、需要重新安檢或託運行李、需要辦理轉機手續或因班機延誤錯過轉機航班等。另外，也要確認是否需要申請簽證。即便是免簽證國家，有些國家還是需要辦理轉機過境簽證。

☆ 轉機的類型

不同的轉機		特色
中途轉機 (中轉)		不用換飛機、不用再安檢、不用再託運行李，因此不用特別預留轉機時間，只要按照航空公司的安排即可。
換機轉	同航空	不用再託運行李，因此不容易出錯。若前一個班機延誤，航空公司也會負責乘客的食宿等費用。
	不同航空	登機證和託運行李通常需要再次辦理；登機時間依各航空公司規定有所不同，因此建議多預留一點時間轉機會比較保險！ ❗ 若為同聯盟的航空公司，辦理程序通常比較輕鬆。
	廉價航空	建議預留至少三到四小時，因為登機證和託運行李都需要重新辦理。 ❗ 大多廉航無保證搭機服務，若是轉機延誤就糟了！
	其他	國際轉國際線、國際轉國內線、國內轉國內線、國內轉國際線，以上轉機方式不盡相同。尤其國際線和國內線通常在不同航廈甚至是不同機場，若行程有安排國際轉國內線時一定要特別留意。

☆ 【轉機必確認】：登機證、行李託運、簽證。

登機證	持有聯程登機證 (onward flight boarding pass)	依指示前往轉機處→通過安全檢查→登機
	沒有聯程登機證	找到轉機櫃臺→辦理登機手續→拿到新的登機證→依指示前往轉機處→通過安全檢查→登機
行李託運	直掛	從出發地到目的地，只需要託運行李一次。
	不能直掛	轉機時，得先領取並再次託運行李，比較費時。(若有轉換機場、轉換國內外航線、航程中包含廉航或轉機時間超過二十四小時等情況，行李通常不能直掛。)
簽證		一定要確認轉機過境國家是否需要簽證，以免買了機票卻上不了飛機。

飛航旅途篇

詢問座位、
放置行李、
更換座位

 字彙出外景

🎧 **06-1**

① captain/pilot *n.* [C] 機長

② first officer (FO)/co-pilot *n.* [C] 副機長

③ cabin crew *n.* [U] 機組人員

④ flight attendant *n.* [C] 空服員

⑤ aboard *adv.* 登機

⑥ straight *adv.* 直地

⑦ ahead *adv.* 在前面

⑧ seat number *n.* [C] 座位號碼

⑨ front-row seat *n.* [C] 前排座位

⑩ back-row seat *n.* [C] 後排座位

⑪ room *n.* [U] 空間

⑫ stow *vt.* 妥善放置

⑬ underneath *prep.* 在…下面

⑭ overhead bin/compartment
n. [C] 上方行李置物箱

⑮ fasten *vt.* 繫好

⑯ move over *phr.* 挪動

⑰ exchange *vt.* 交換

⑱ switch *vt.* 調換

Donna is talking with a flight attendant.

Attendant: Welcome aboard. May I help you?

Donna: Yes, could you show me where my seat is?

Attendant: May I see your boarding pass, please?

Donna: No problem. (*Showing her boarding pass*)

Attendant: This way, please. Go straight ahead. It's a window seat on your right.

唐娜正在和一位空服員談話。

空服員：歡迎登機。有什麼是我可以幫你的嗎？

唐娜：有的，可以麻煩你告訴我我的座位在哪裡嗎？

空服員：可以看一下你的登機證嗎？

唐娜：沒問題。(*出示她的登機證*)

空服員：這邊請。向前直走。是在你右邊的靠窗座位。

Andrew is talking with another passenger, Ruby.

Andrew: Excuse me. Is this seat 32B?

Ruby: Yes, it is.

Andrew: I'm afraid you're in my seat.

Ruby: Let me check my boarding pass. Oh, my seat number is 33B. It's in the next row. Sorry, my fault.

Andrew: No worries.

安德魯正在和另一位乘客露比談話。

安德魯：不好意思。這個座位是 32B 嗎？

露比：是的。

安德魯：恐怕你坐了我的位子。

露比：我看一下我的登機證。喔，我的座位號碼是 33B。是在後面一排。抱歉，我坐錯了。

安德魯：沒關係。

 06-4

A flight attendant is moving over to let Doris take her seat.

Attendant: Excuse me, ma'am. I'm afraid your bag has to be stowed in the overhead bin or underneath the seat in front of you.

Doris: Alright. Could you help me put it in the overhead bin?

Attendant: No problem, ma'am.

一位空服員正在挪動位置讓朵莉絲就座。

空服員：抱歉，女士。恐怕你需要將包包放上方行李置物箱或你前面座位的下方。

朵莉絲：好的。你可以幫我把它放進上方行李置物箱嗎？

空服員：沒問題，女士。

06-5

Sean is talking with a flight attendant.

Sean: Excuse me, would it be possible to switch seats? My friend and I would like to sit together.

Attendant: Sure, sir, but for now, please take your seat. The "fasten seat belt" sign is on. Once the sign is off, I'll help you with that.

Sean: OK. Thank you.

尚恩正在和一位空服員談話。

尚恩：不好意思，請問有可能換位子嗎？我朋友和我想要坐在一起。

空服員：當然可以，先生，但是現在請你先就座。「繫安全帶」指示燈已經開啟。一旦指示燈關閉，我會幫你換位子。

尚恩：好的。謝謝。

還能這樣說

1. It's a window seat on your right.

> a middle seat 中間的座位
>
> a window seat on the left 左邊靠窗的位子
>
> an aisle seat on your right 你右邊靠走道的位子
>
> over there, in the left aisle 在那裡，在左邊的走道

2. I'm afraid you're in my seat.

> this is my seat 這是我的位子
>
> you have my seat 你坐了我的位子
>
> 32B is my seat 32B是我的位子

現在才知道

機上座椅小百科 🔍

☆ 常見的配置

1. armrest 扶手
2. backrest 靠背
3. seat belt 安全帶
4. seat pocket 座椅置物袋
5. seatback screen 座椅螢幕
6. reading light (switch) 閱讀燈 (開關)

7. AC outlet AC 插座
8. USB port USB 插座
9. headphones 頭戴式耳機
10. flight attendant call button 空服員呼喚鈕
11. in-seat power outlet 座椅電源插座

☆ 如何搶到最佳座位

1. 提早買機票：越早買票越有機會選到你心目中的最佳座位，但可能需付費選位。
2. 提早劃位：早起的鳥兒有蟲吃，要留意航空公司開放網路預辦登機的時間，越早辦理越有機會選到好機位。
3. 加入航空公司的會員：航空公司通常會提供會員較多服務與優惠，例如：哩程累積、優先辦理登機手續、優先升等艙位、使用機場貴賓室及使用哩程累積免費選位等。

☆ 如何選擇最佳飛機座位

1. 座位編號：一般較寬的航班橫向座位會用 ABC-DEFG-HJK 來表示，A 和 K 代表靠窗座位，C、D、G 和 H 代表走道座位。較窄的航班 (例如：廉價航空的輕型客機) 的橫向座位則以 ABC-DEF 表示，A 和 F 是靠窗座位，C 和 D 是走道座位。因此可依據編號，選擇個人偏好的座位。

 你沒看錯，沒有字母 I！這是為了避免與數字 1 搞混喔！

2. 最安全的座位：根據統計，不幸發生意外時，靠近飛機尾部的乘客存活率較高。

3. 最好睡的座位：最好睡的座位是機艙中部左側的靠窗座位。因為航程中飛機向左傾斜的機率較大，乘客可以靠著機身休息。此外，也可避免起身讓鄰座乘客進出的困擾。

4. 最穩的座位：遇到亂流時，與機翼齊平的座位其顛簸幅度會較其他座位小。

5. 最吵的座位：因為離飛機的引擎最近，機翼旁的座位最吵。靠窗座位則因風噪的關係而較吵。若考量乘客走動頻率，靠近洗手間、廚房、機艙門和走道的座位會比較吵。

6. 最便宜的大座位：因空間配置的關係，經濟艙第一排和緊急出口旁邊的走道座位的腿部空間通常較大。但這類座位通常會預留給行動不便或有帶嬰兒的乘客。若一般人要預選此座位，可能需付費或加入該航空公司的會員。

飛航旅途篇

機上用餐、
機上購物、
意見反應

 字彙出外景

🎧 07-1

① airline/in-flight meal *n.* [C] 飛機餐

② vegetarian meal *n.* [C] 素食餐

③ infant/child meal *n.* [C] 嬰兒／兒童餐

④ blanket *n.* [C] 毛毯

⑤ beverage *n.* [C] 飲料

⑥ tray table *n.* [C] 摺疊桌

⑦ tableware *n.* [U] 餐具

⑧ in-flight shopping *n.* [U] 機上購物

⑨ duty-free *adj.* (商品) 免稅的

⑩ goods *n.* (*pl.*) 商品

⑪ discount *n.* [C] 打折

⑫ item *n.* [C] 商品

⑬ snore *vi.* 打鼾

⑭ restriction *n.* [C] 限制

⑮ receipt *n.* [C] 收據，發票

旅遊狀況句

07-2

Scott is talking with a flight attendant.

Attendant: Excuse me, sir. Could you return your seat to the upright position and put down your tray table, please?

Scott: Oh, sure.

Attendant: What would you like for dinner, fish or chicken?

Scott: Chicken, please.

Attendant: Here you are. Anything to drink?

Scott: Coke, please.

Attendant: OK. Here you are.

史考特正在和一位空服員談話。

空服員：不好意思，先生。可以請你把座椅豎直並放下摺疊桌嗎？

史考特：喔，當然可以。

空服員：你晚餐要吃什麼，魚肉還是雞肉？

史考特：請給我雞肉。

空服員：這給你。要喝什麼飲料嗎？

史考特：請給我可樂。

空服員：好的。這給你。

07-3

Ella is talking with a flight attendant.

Attendant: Duty-free goods?

Ella: Excuse me. Is there any discount on Chanel perfumes?

Attendant: If you buy two bottles, you can get another one 40% off.

Ella: I see. I'll take these three bottles, please.

Attendant: OK. Will that be all, ma'am?

Ella: Yes, that's everything.

艾拉正在和一位空服員談話。

空服員：需要免稅商品嗎？

艾拉：不好意思，請問香奈兒香水有折扣嗎？

空服員：如果你買兩瓶，第三瓶打六折。

艾拉：了解。請給我這三瓶。

空服員：好的。就這些嗎，女士？

艾拉：是的，就這些。

 購買機場或機上免稅品時，記得要特別留意轉機及入境國家的安全檢查容量限制及報關須知喔！

 07-4

Warner is talking with a flight attendant.

Warner: Excuse me, my headphones aren't working. I can't hear anything.

Attendant: I'm sorry. I'll get you a new set.

Warner: Thank you. (*Whispering*) By the way, could you bring me a pair of earplugs, please? The passenger in the front row snores so loudly that I can't fall asleep.

Attendant: Certainly. I'll be right back.

華納正在和一位空服員談話。

華納：不好意思，我的耳機壞了。我聽不到聲音。

空服員：很抱歉。我會拿一副新的給你。

華納：謝謝。(*低語*) 順帶一提，可以請你給我一副耳塞嗎？前排的乘客打鼾很大聲，以致於我無法入睡。

空服員：當然。我馬上回來。

還能這樣說

1. What would you like for dinner, fish or chicken?

> breakfast 早餐
> lunch 午餐
> snack/refreshments 點心

> beef or pork 牛肉或豬肉
> rice or noodles 飯或麵
> chicken with rice or noodles
> 雞肉飯或雞肉麵
> cookies or mixed nuts and raisins
> 餅乾或綜合堅果和葡萄乾

2. Coke, please.

> Water 水
> Coffee 咖啡
> Cocktail 雞尾酒
> Ginger ale 薑汁汽水

> Apple/Orange juice 蘋果／柳橙汁
> Green/Black/Oolong tea 綠／紅／烏龍茶
> Red/White wine 紅／白酒
> Sprite/7 Up/(Diet) Coke 雪碧／七喜／(健怡) 可樂

3. Could you bring me a pair of earplugs, please?

> bring me another blanket 再給我一條毛毯
> clear my tray table 清理我的摺疊桌
> refill my coffee/tea/water 幫我添加咖啡／茶／水
> show me where the lavatory is 告訴我廁所在哪裡
> help me fill out this form 幫我填寫這張表格
> show me how to use the remote (control) 教我如何使用遙控器

現在才知道

飛機上的好吃好玩 🔍

☆ 飛機餐這樣選準沒錯

1. 優先選米飯：飛機餐是事先做好的餐盒，上機後再次加熱。二次加熱後麵條會黏成一團，而米飯會保持濕潤。

2. 優先選雞肉：二次加熱後，豬肉和牛肉會變得乾柴、海鮮則會不夠新鮮，而雞肉的口感相對而言會比其他肉類要好。

3. 優先選咖哩：在乾燥又低壓的機艙環境，味蕾對甜味及鹹味食物的敏感度會降低約百分之三十，所以選擇重口味餐點可以讓人胃口大開。

4. 依據航空公司選餐：歐美航空公司的西餐通常做得比中餐好，而亞洲航空公司則是中餐比較好吃。

5. 提早訂特別餐：若因身體或宗教信仰等因素而有特殊飲食習慣，可以在訂機票時一併預訂餐點。

6. 主動要求飲料：除了常見的茶飲、咖啡、果汁和汽水外，國際航班通常還會提供啤酒、紅酒、白酒甚至香檳等，而這類酒精飲料通常要乘客主動詢問才會提供。

7. 再來一份：飛機上的配餐數量通常會比實際乘客數稍微多幾份，因此用餐後還是肚子餓時，可以詢問空服員是否可以再要一份。

☆ 機上娛樂 (in-flight entertainment)

除了餐飲服務，航空公司還會提供機上娛樂讓乘客打發時間。

常見的機上娛樂有：

1. 影片／音訊娛樂：乘客可透過個人螢幕觀賞各式電影、電視節目或音樂。

2. 電子遊戲：除了單機遊戲，部分航班甚至支援機上乘客間的對戰遊戲。此外，也有益智型遊戲供乘客打發時間。

3. 動態地圖：乘客可以透過螢幕即時觀察飛機目前的位置、航線、飛行速度、高度、風速、艙外溫度、飛行時間、目的地距離和當地時間等資訊。有些也會提供機艙外畫面，例如：起飛和降落的畫面。

4. 機上 Wi-Fi：乘客可使用機上 Wi-Fi 連接網際網路 (目前大多需付費使用)。

飛航旅途篇

機上廣播——
起降、亂流、
安全示範

 字彙出外景

08-1

❶ take-off *n.* [C][U] 起飛

❷ aircraft *n.* [C] 飛機

❸ electronic device *n.* [C] 電子設備

❹ airplane/flight mode *n.* [U] 飛行模式

❺ escape hatch/emergency exit

   n. [C] 緊急出口

❻ smoke detector *n.* [C] 煙霧偵測器

❼ forbid *vt.* 禁止

❽ turbulence *n.* [U] 亂流

❾ secure *vt.* 扣緊

❿ suspend *vt.* 暫停

⓫ cooperation *n.* [U] 配合

⓬ safety demonstration *n.* [C] 安全示範

⓭ life vest/jacket *n.* [C] 救生衣

⓮ oxygen mask *n.* [C] 氧氣面罩

⓯ turn/switch on/off *phr.* 開啟／關閉(電器)

⓰ inflate *vi.*; *vt.* 使充氣

⓱ buckle *vi.*; *vt.* 扣上

⓲ descend *vi.* 降落

旅遊英文 這樣就GO

旅遊狀況句

🎧 08-2

(In-flight announcement)

Good morning, ladies and gentlemen. Welcome aboard Flight CX201 with service from Taipei to Los Angeles. We are currently third in line for take-off and are expected to be in the air in approximately twenty minutes. Please fasten your seat belts and return your seats and tray tables to the upright position. Be sure to switch all personal electronic devices to airplane mode. As a reminder, smoking is prohibited in any area of the aircraft, including the lavatories. Disabling or destroying lavatory smoke detectors is forbidden by law. Thank you for choosing Top Airlines. Enjoy your flight.

(機上廣播)

早安，各位女士、先生們。歡迎搭乘臺北飛往洛杉磯的 CX201 航班。我們目前排在起飛的第三順位，預計將在大約二十分鐘後起飛。請你繫好安全帶、豎直椅背並收妥摺疊桌。確保將所有個人電子設備調為飛航模式。提醒你，飛機上所有區域都禁止吸菸，包括廁所。法律禁止讓廁所煙霧偵測器失效或損毀。感謝你搭乘頂尖航空。祝你飛行愉快。

08-3

(In-flight announcement)

Ladies and gentlemen, the captain has turned on the "fasten seat belt" sign as we are crossing a zone of turbulence now. Please return to your seats, keep your seat belts fastened, secure your tray tables, and place your seats in the upright position. And the lavatories should not be used until the sign is turned off. Cabin service will be suspended during this period. Thank you for your cooperation.

(機上廣播)

各位女士、先生們，由於我們正通過一段不穩定的氣流，機長已開啟「繫安全帶」指示燈。請你回到座位、繫好安全帶、扣緊摺疊桌並豎直椅背。在指示燈熄滅前，請不要使用廁所。客艙服務在這段期間將暫停。感謝你的配合。

08-4

(In-flight announcement)

The oxygen mask will automatically drop above your head when cabin pressure changes suddenly. When it does so, place the mask over your nose and mouth, tighten the straps, and breathe normally. Your life vest is under your seat. First, put it on over your head. Then, buckle and tighten the waist straps. Pull the handle and your life vest will automatically inflate. If it doesn't fill, please blow into the tube in front. Please inflate your vest only when you are leaving the emergency exit. For more information, please refer to your safety instruction card or ask the flight attendants. Thank you.

(機上廣播)

當機艙氣壓突然改變時，氧氣面罩會自動從你的上方落下。發生此情況時，請將面罩罩住口、鼻，調整鬆緊帶並正常呼吸。救生衣在你的座椅下方。首先將其從頭上套下。之後，扣好並拉緊腰帶。拉下手把，救生衣將自動充氣。若沒有充氣，請吹氣進前方管子。請於離開緊急出口時再充氣。如需更多資訊，請你參閱安全指示卡或詢問空服員。謝謝。

08-5

(In-flight announcement)

Ladies and gentlemen, we will be landing at Narita International Airport in a short while. The local time now is 2:00 p.m. The ground temperature is 20 degrees Celsius or 68 degrees Fahrenheit. We will soon end the in-flight entertainment service, and our flight attendants will be collecting your headphones.

(機上廣播)

各位女士、先生們，我們即將降落在成田國際機場。現在當地時間是下午兩點。地面溫度攝氏二十度，華氏六十八度。我們很快會停止機上娛樂服務，而我們的空服員會收回耳機。

還能這樣說

1. Please fasten your seat belts and return your seats and tray tables to the upright position.

take your assigned seats 按指定的座位入座
keep the window shades open during take-off or landing
起飛或降落期間，遮陽板請保持開啟

2. Be sure to switch all personal electronic devices to airplane mode.

turn off all personal electronic devices 關掉所有個人電子設備
switch off your cellphones 關掉你的手機

3. Smoking is prohibited in any area of the aircraft.

not allowed/permitted for the duration of the flight 航程期間都不被允許

現在才知道

機上廣播大補帖 🔍

1. 起飛前廣播：提醒乘客將隨身物品置於座位上方的行李置物箱內或前面座椅的下方。此外，有些國家不允許乘客在起飛時使用任何個人電子設備 (包括有飛航模式的電子產品)，乘客得仔細聆聽並遵守各國規定。有些航空公司為了避免意外發生，也會提醒乘客不要使用鋰電池行動電源為電子設備充電，並全程關閉行動電源。

2. 起飛後廣播：通常是由機長廣播，歡迎乘客搭機後，會告知目前巡航高度 (例如：cruising at an altitude of 35,000 feet)、天氣狀況、預計抵達目的地的時間、飛行時間等航班資訊或客艙服務開始的時間。

3. 亂流廣播：提醒乘客應盡快回到座位並繫好安全帶，避免意外發生。如果不能及時回到座位，可以抓緊行李置物箱邊緣的凹槽處；如果正在使用廁所，可抓緊廁所內的扶手。如果身體因亂流而感到不適，可以與空服員聯繫。

4. 安全示範廣播：內容包含救生衣上的指示燈遇水會自動發亮 (water-activated locator light)、救生衣上的哨子可以用來吸引救援人員的注意、緊急逃生時不要攜帶任何隨身物品、不要穿高跟鞋、不要配戴尖銳物品、要按照緊急照明燈 (emergency light) 的指示前往最近的緊急出口、艙門外會有充氣滑梯 (inflatable slide) 等相關逃生訊息。此外，在緊急狀況時，乘客應採取準備迫降姿勢 (brace position) (身體前傾、雙手抱頭及手肘放在大腿上)，盡可能地保護自己。

 相關影片可至 YouTube 搜尋「機上安全影片」喔！

5. 降落廣播：再次提醒乘客豎直椅背、收起摺疊桌、繫好安全帶、打開遮陽板並將電子設備關閉或調成飛航模式，此時也可能會提供預計抵達時間等。

6. 降落後廣播：飛機降落後，會提醒乘客在飛機完全停止前不要解開安全帶、不要離開座位和不要使用手機。待飛機完全停下後，再提醒乘客提取行李時要小心行李掉落 (飛行過程中，行李可能會位移)。空服員也會提醒乘客要記得帶隨身行李，不要遺落在飛機上，託運行李要到行李提領處領取，需要轉機的乘客要到轉機櫃臺辦理。最後，感謝乘客選擇搭乘該航班，期待乘客再度搭乘並表達祝福。

安心住宿篇

Unit
09

預訂飯店、
更換房間、
入住手續

 字彙出外景

🎧 **09-1**

❶ reserve *vt.* 預訂

❷ room reservation *n.* [C] 預訂房間

❸ room rate *n.* [C] 房價

❹ deposit *n.* [C] 訂金

❺ room type *n.* [C] 房型

❻ vacancy *n.* [C] 空房

❼ check in/out

　phr. (飯店) 辦理入住／退房手續

❽ check-in/out time

　n. [U] 入住／退房時間

❾ arrange *vt.* 安排

❿ overnight *adv.* 一晚

⓫ per *prep.* 每

⓬ lobby *n.* [C] (飯店) 大廳

⓭ reception (desk)/front desk

　n. [U] (飯店) 櫃臺

⓮ receptionist/front desk agent

　n. [C] (飯店櫃臺) 接待員

⓯ bellboy/bellhop *n.* [C] 門僮，行李員

⓰ key card *n.* [C] 房卡

🎧 09-2

Ramon is calling a hotel to make a room reservation.

Ramon: Hello. I'd like to book a room, please.

Receptionist: What date will you be arriving?

Ramon: On May 1st.

Receptionist: How long are you going to stay?

Ramon: We'll only stay overnight.

Receptionist: What kind of room would you like?

Ramon: I'd like to reserve a double room.

Receptionist: It's NT$2,500 per night. There's a 10% deposit on the room. Is that OK?

Ramon: It's OK.

Receptionist: No problem, sir. We can arrange a double room for you on the day you requested. May I have your name and phone number, please?

雷蒙正在打電話到飯店預訂房間。

雷蒙：你好。我想要預訂房間。

接待員：請問你要於哪天入住？

雷蒙：五月一日。

接待員：你要入住幾天呢？

雷蒙：我們只住一晚。

接待員：你想要哪一種房型？

雷蒙：我想預訂一間雙人房。

接待員：雙人房每晚新臺幣 2,500 元。預訂房間要收 10% 的訂金。可以嗎？

雷蒙：好的。

接待員：沒問題，先生。我們會在你要求的那一天安排一間雙人房給你。可以給我你的姓名和電話號碼嗎？

🎧 09-3

Vicki is calling a hotel to make changes to her reservation.

Vicki: Hello. My name is Vicki Jones. I'd like to change my reservation for June 9th. I've booked a single, but I'd like to change the room type to a double, if possible.

Receptionist: Alright, Ms. Jones. We have a double room available on June 9th, but it will cost NT$1,000 more than the single one.

Vicki: That won't be a problem. I'll take it.

Receptionist: OK, Ms. Jones. We'll make the change for you.

維琪正在打電話到飯店修改住宿訂單。

維琪：你好，我的名字是維琪・瓊斯。我想更改我六月九日的預訂。我訂了一間單人房，但如果可以的話，我想將房型改為雙人房。

接待員：好的，瓊斯小姐。我們六月九日還有一間雙人房，但是比單人房貴新臺幣 1,000 元。

維琪：那沒問題。給我一間。

接待員：好的，瓊斯小姐。我們會為你更改。

 09-4

Josh is checking in at the reception. A bellboy is carrying Josh's suitcase and waiting in the lobby.

Receptionist: Good afternoon. How may I help you?

Josh: Hi, I've booked a single room online for tonight.

Receptionist: May I have your name and reservation number, please?

Josh: Josh Edwards. The number is 8463037.

Receptionist: Alright, Mr. Edwards. You have reserved a single for one night. May I have your passport?

Josh: There you are.

Receptionist: OK, Mr. Edwards. Here is your passport and key card. You will be in Room 608 on the 6th floor.

喬許正在櫃臺辦理入住手續。行李員正帶著喬許的行李在大廳等候。

接待員：午安。有什麼能為你服務的嗎？

喬許：嗨，我在網上訂了一間今天晚上的單人房。

接待員：請問你的名字和訂房號碼是？

喬許：喬許・愛德華茲。號碼是 8463037。

接待員：好的，愛德華茲先生。你預訂了一晚的單人房。可以給我你的護照嗎？

喬許：這邊。

接待員：好的，愛德華茲先生。這是你的護照和房卡。你的房間是六樓的 608 號房。

還能這樣說

1. I'd like to book/reserve a room, please.

single room 單人房	triple room 三人房
double room 雙人房	quadruple room 四人房
twin room 雙床雙人房	family suit 家庭套房

2. How long are you going to stay?

How many nights are you going to stay? 你要住幾晚呢？

How long/many nights do you intend to stay? 你預計要住多久／幾晚？

How long/many nights will you be staying? 你要住多久／幾晚？

When will you be leaving? 你預計何時要離開呢？

現在才知道

飯店訂房小知識 🔍

☆ 常見的飯店房型

1. 單人房 (single room)：房間有一張單人床，房間較小但價錢比雙人房便宜。

2. 雙人房分為：

(1) 單床雙人房 (double room)：房間有一張雙人床。

(2) 雙床雙人房 (twin room)：房間有兩張單人床。

(3) 半雙人房 (semi-double room)：常見於日本的房型，房間有一張尺寸介於單人及雙人床之間的床，身材高大的人可能會覺得空間比較不足。

3. 三人房 (triple room)：房間有三張單人床或是一張雙人床加一張單人床。

☆ 訂房注意事項

1. 不要少報入住人數：除了可能會被要求多加錢外，也有消防安全的風險。

2. 飯店沒有三人房，但有三人要入住：可以試試雙人房加一床，價格通常會比訂一間雙人房加一間單人房便宜。但不是所有飯店都有提供加床服務，因此要事先詢問清楚喔。

3. 對菸味很敏感：可以選擇禁菸房 (non-smoking room)。

4. 想要有景觀：可以選擇有花園景觀／海景／山景的房型 (a room with a(n) garden/ocean/mountain view)。

5. 關於早餐的對話：

(1) Is breakfast included in the room rate?/
Does this charge include breakfast?
房價有包含早餐費用嗎？

(2) What time is breakfast served at? 早餐幾點開始供應？

6. 關於接送服務的對話：

Do you have a shuttle bus service to the airport/train station?
你們有提供到機場／火車站的接送服務嗎？

☆ 辦理入住／寄放行李

1. 辦理入住手續時，服務人員會請房客填寫登記卡 (registration card/form)，內容通常為姓名、電話、居住地址等訊息，最後通常也會請顧客簽名。

2. 關於寄放行李時的對話：

(1) May I leave my baggage here?
我可以將行李留在這邊嗎？

🛈 很多人出國遊玩時喜歡坐早班機，而一般飯店的入住時間是下午三點之後。若不想拎著大包小包旅行，就可以先到飯店寄放行李喔！

(2) Since I have a late flight, can I store my baggage at the hotel until 6:00 p.m.?
因為我搭的是晚班機，我可以將行李寄放在飯店到六點嗎？

🛈 退房時，如果去機場的時間還早，也可以辦理延遲退房或先將行李寄放在飯店當天晚點再取回。

安心住宿篇

飯店服務：
喚醒服務、
索取物品、
房間整理、
房內設備
異常

 字彙出外景

🎧 10-1

❶ wake-up call *n.* [C] 喚醒服務

❷ housekeeping *n.* [U] (飯店) 房務部門

❸ housekeeper *n.* [C] 房務清潔人員

❹ supply *vt.* 提供

❺ minibar *n.* [C] 迷你吧

❻ curtain *n.* [C] 窗簾

❼ sheet *n.* [C] 床單

❽ pillow *n.* [C] 枕頭

❾ slipper *n.* [C] 拖鞋

❿ bath towel *n.* [C] 浴巾

⓫ bath mat *n.* [C] 浴室地墊

⓬ toilet *n.* [C] 馬桶

⓭ faucet *n.* [C] 水龍頭

⓮ showerhead *n.* [C] 蓮蓬頭

⓯ mess *n.* [C] 雜亂，不整潔

⓰ broken *adj.* 損壞的

⓱ maintenance *n.* [U] 維修

旅遊狀況句

🎧 10-2

Gary is calling a receptionist to ask for a wake-up call.

Gary: Hello. I'm in Room 512. I'd like a wake-up call tomorrow morning.

Receptionist: Of course, sir. At what time should we call you?

Gary: Make it five in the morning. I need to catch a flight.

Receptionist: No problem. We'll give you a call then.

蓋瑞正在打電話給飯店櫃臺接待員要求喚醒服務。

蓋瑞：你好。我在 512 號房。我明天早上想要喚醒服務。

接待員：當然，先生。我們應該幾點叫醒你？

蓋瑞：早上五點鐘。我要趕飛機。

接待員：沒問題。我們到時會打電話給你。

🎧 10-3

Vera is calling a receptionist in her room.

Vera: This is Room 1315. My bath towel is accidentally wet. Would you please bring me another one?

Receptionist: Certainly, ma'am. I will ask housekeeping to supply you with a fresh towel. Do you need anything else?

Vera: I'd like an extra pillow.

Receptionist: No problem.

維拉正在她的房間撥打電話給飯店櫃臺接待員。

維拉：這是 1315 號房。我的浴巾不小心濕了。你們可以再送一條上來給我嗎？

接待員：當然，女士。我會請房務部門提供新的浴巾給你。你還需要什麼嗎？

維拉：我想多要一個枕頭。

接待員：沒問題。

🎧 **10-4**

Philip is speaking to a receptionist on the phone.

Receptionist: Front desk. What can I do for you?

Philip: This is Mr. Brown in Room 803. My room hasn't been serviced. The sheets are dirty, and the bed hasn't been made. The bathroom is also in a mess.

Receptionist: I'm terribly sorry to hear that. It should have been done this morning. I'll call the housekeeper immediately.

菲利普正在跟一位飯店櫃臺接待員講電話。

接待員：這裡是櫃臺。有什麼可以幫你的嗎？

菲利普：這裡是 803 號房的布朗先生。我的房間還沒打掃。床單很髒，而且床沒鋪好。浴室也一團亂。

接待員：我非常抱歉聽到這狀況。今天早上應該就要打掃好的。我會立刻打電話給房務員。

🎧 **10-5**

Alison is speaking to a receptionist on the phone.

Alison: The TV in our room is broken.

Receptionist: I'm sorry. May I have your room number, please? I'll send someone to check it soon.

Alison: I'm in Room 742, but I'll go out in a moment.

Receptionist: Alright, I'll let the maintenance staff know.

艾莉森正在跟一位飯店櫃臺接待員講電話。

艾莉森：我們房間裡的電視壞了。

接待員：很抱歉。可以給我你的房號嗎？我會盡快派人去檢查。

艾莉森：我在 742 號房，但是我等一下就要出去。

接待員：好的，我會讓維修員知道。

還能這樣說

1. The TV in our room is broken.

shampoo 洗髮精 conditioner 潤髮乳 bath gel 沐浴乳 body lotion 乳液 razor 刮鬍刀 shower cap 浴帽 toothpaste 牙膏 toothbrush 牙刷 tissue/toilet paper 面紙／衛生紙	has run out 用完了
air conditioner 冷氣 phone 電話 electric kettle 電熱水壺 safe deposit box 保險箱 hairdryer 吹風機 bulb 燈泡	makes a funny noise 發出奇怪的聲音 doesn't work/ is out of order/ is not working 壞了 has burned out 燒壞了
toilet 馬桶 faucet 水龍頭 bathroom sink 浴室洗臉盆 bathtub 浴缸 Jacuzzi 按摩浴缸	doesn't flush 不能沖水 is leaking 漏水 seems to be clogged/plugged up 似乎堵住了

2. I'll send someone/the maintenance staff to check it soon.

look into 仔細檢查　　　take care of 處理　　　take a look at 看一看

現在才知道

客房服務好方便 🔍

☆ 客房服務

1. 一般服務：包含更換床單、鋪床、夜床服務、清潔地板、整理房間、清理廁所、更換毛巾、補充各項客房用品、客房餐飲服務和洗衣服務等。

> ❗ 隨著環保意識抬頭，有些飯店會提供卡片，讓住客放在床上或毛巾架子上，以告知房務清潔人員不需要每天更換床單或毛巾。

2. 夜床服務 (turndown service)：若下午五點到六點房客尚未回到客房，房務員會先將房間內的窗簾放下、掀開床頭棉被一角並拍鬆枕頭，營造出適合入睡的氛圍，有些星級飯店甚至還會準備熱飲、點心或香氛精油。

☆ 其他服務

1. 充電器 (charger) 與轉接頭 (adapter)：出遊一趟，身上總是會攜帶一些需要充電的裝置，例如：手機、相機、筆電、平板電腦或行動電源等。如果充電相關配件忘記帶或者不夠用時，都可以詢問飯店是否能借用。

2. 電暖氣 (heater) ／加濕器 (humidifier) ／空氣清淨機 (air purifier)：若空氣太冷、太乾、太濕或者有異味，都可以詢問飯店是否有提供相應的電器喔。

3. 寢具：如果棉被不夠用或枕頭太扁或太軟時，可以詢問飯店是否能提供額外的寢具。有些飯店甚至提供各式枕頭供住客挑選。

4. 衣物：行李箱衣物難免碰撞，若衣服變得皺巴巴該怎麼辦？雖然飯店無法免費幫你整燙衣物，但是你可以和飯店借用熨斗 (iron) 喔！若衣物的鈕扣不小心脫落，有些飯店也有提供簡易的針線組 (sewing kit)。

5. 噪音干擾：客房隔音不好還是隔壁住客講話太大聲，吵得你受不了嗎？可以向飯店索取耳塞，或者通知飯店人員請他們協助處理噪音問題。

6. 雨具：忘記帶雨傘也不用怕，通常飯店有提供愛心傘供住客借用，有些甚至還提供輕便雨衣。

7. 免費的備品：房內提供的盥洗用品 (例如：牙刷、個人裝沐浴乳及洗髮精等) 及沖泡飲品等，通常都可以於退房時帶走。

 特別注意：飯店的毛巾不能帶走喔！有些飯店迷你吧提供的飲料和零食並不是免費取用的，因此要特別留意有沒有價目表喔！

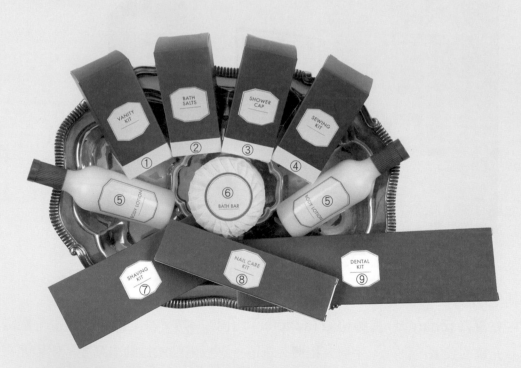

① 護理套裝 (棉花棒、化妝棉等)　　⑥ 香皂

② 浴鹽　　　　　　　　　　　　　⑦ 刮鬍組

③ 浴帽　　　　　　　　　　　　　⑧ 修甲組

④ 針線組　　　　　　　　　　　　⑨ 牙刷組

⑤ 乳液

安心住宿篇

飯店服務：
飯店設施、
洗衣服務、
房卡相關、
房內用餐

 字彙出外景

🎧 **11-1**

❶ provide *vt.* 提供

❷ amenity *n.* [C] (*usu. pl.*) (娛樂) 便利設施

❸ facilities *n.* (*pl.*) 設施，設備

❹ gym *n.* [C] 健身房

❺ spa *n.* [C] 水療中心

❻ sauna *n.* [C] 蒸氣室，桑拿室

❼ work out *phr.* 鍛鍊身體

❽ relax *vi.* 放鬆

❾ Wi-Fi *n.* [U] 無線網路

❿ Internet access *n.* [U] 網路連線

⓫ pick up *phr.* 拿，取

⓬ deliver *vt.* 遞送

⓭ laundry *n.* [U] 待洗的或洗好的衣服

⓮ laundry service *n.* [U] 洗衣服務

⓯ laundry bag *n.* [C] 洗衣袋

⓰ laundry form *n.* [C] 洗衣單

⓱ lock sb out (of sth) *phr.* 將…鎖在 (…) 外

⓲ room service *n.* [U] 客房餐飲服務

🎧 11-2

Robin is talking with a receptionist.

Robin: What about your amenities? Do you have a pool?

Receptionist: Yes, we have an indoor swimming pool. We also have a gym, a spa and a sauna for you to work out and relax.

Robin: That's great! What about Wi-Fi?

Receptionist: We provide our guests with Internet access.

羅賓正在和一位飯店櫃臺接待員談話。

羅賓：你們有什麼設施？有游泳池嗎？

接待員：有的，我們有一座室內游泳池。我們也有健身房、水療中心和蒸氣室供你健身及放鬆。

羅賓：太好了！那有無線網路嗎？

接待員：我們提供網路連線給房客。

🎧 11-3

Annabelle, a hotel guest, is calling housekeeping.

Housekeeper: Housekeeping. May I help you?

Annabelle: I have a skirt and a pair of pants that need to be cleaned.

Housekeeper: OK. I'll send someone to pick up your laundry right away.

Annabelle: Thank you. By the way, when will they be ready?

Housekeeper: We will deliver your laundry by noon tomorrow.

飯店房客安娜貝爾正在打電話給房務部門。

房務人員：房務部門。有什麼是我可以幫你的嗎？

安娜貝爾：我有一件裙子和一條褲子要洗。

房務人員：好的，我馬上派人去取你要洗的衣物。

安娜貝爾：謝謝。對了，什麼時候會洗好？

房務人員：我們明天中午前會送回你送洗的衣物。

11-4

Terry is talking with a receptionist.

Terry: Hi, I'm Terry Simpson in Room 1617. I left the key card in my room. I can't get in now.

Receptionist: May I see your passport, Mr. Simpson?

Terry: Here you are.

Receptionist: OK. My colleague will go up with you and open the door.

泰瑞正在和一位飯店櫃臺接待員談話。

泰瑞：嗨，我是住在 1617 號房的泰瑞・辛普森。我把房卡留在我的房間裡了。我現在進不去。

接待員：可以看一下你的護照嗎，辛普森先生？

泰瑞：給你。

接待員：好的。我的同事會陪同你上樓並開門。

 11-5

Nick, a hotel guest, is ordering breakfast from room service.

Nick: Hello. This is Room 908. I'd like to order something to eat. Could you please send up an American breakfast?

Receptionist: Certainly, sir. Will that be all?

Nick: Yes, that's all. Could you get everything ready within twenty minutes? I'm in a hurry to leave.

Receptionist: No problem.

飯店房客尼克正在跟客房餐飲服務點早餐。

尼克：你好，這裡是 908 號房。我想點餐。可以請你們送一份美式早餐上來嗎？

服務人員：當然可以，先生。這些就行了嗎？

尼克：對，就這樣。你們可以在二十分鐘內準備好嗎？我很快就要出門。

服務人員：沒問題。

還能這樣說

1. I have a skirt and a pair of pants that need to be cleaned.

some shirts 幾件襯衫
a suit 一套西裝
a sweater 一件毛衣
a cardigan 一件開襟毛衣
a jacket 一件夾克

dry-cleaned 乾洗
ironed 熨燙
cleaned by hand in cold water 冷水手洗

2. Could you please send up an American breakfast?

an English breakfast 英式早餐   a continental breakfast 歐陸早餐

美式早餐	英式早餐	歐陸早餐
蛋、培根香腸或火腿、鬆餅、薯餅或薯條	蛋、香腸、煙燻培根、煎厚片番茄、蘑菇、燉豆子、煎吐司	果醬、水果、烤麵包或派

常見的餐點選擇
飲料類：咖啡 (coffee)、果汁 (juice)、茶 (tea)
麵包類：吐司 (toast)、鬆餅 (pancake)、格子鬆餅 (waffle)、可頌麵包 (croissant)
肉類：培根 (bacon)、火腿 (ham)、香腸 (sausage)
蛋類：煎蛋捲 (omelet)、炒蛋 (scrambled eggs)、水煮蛋 (boiled egg)、水波蛋 (poached egg)、太陽蛋 (sunny-side-up egg)、半／全熟荷包蛋 (over easy/hard egg)

現在才知道

免費 Wi-Fi 安全嗎？

現代生活離不開網路，飯店、餐廳、大眾運輸工具等公共場所都有提供免費 Wi-Fi。但是你知道駭客可能會透過這些免費 Wi-Fi 入侵個人手機或電腦竊取個人資料嗎？要如何才能用得安心呢？

1. 注意真假 Wi-Fi：Wi-Fi 的名稱通常即為飯店名稱，而駭客可能編造雷同的 Wi-Fi 名稱來以假亂真，例如：真正的 Wi-Fi 名稱是 Pacifichotel，駭客可能會用 Pacifichotel2 來誘導你使用。所以在連接免費 Wi-Fi 前，可以先跟飯店人員確認正確的 Wi-Fi 名稱。

2. 小心可疑的連結或軟體：不要隨意點擊、安裝可疑的連結或軟體，因為駭客可能藉此將惡意程式植入你的個人手機或電腦。

3. 使用 VPN (Virtual Private Network)：就是指虛擬私人網路，它會將你的網路流量加密，來保護你在網路上的個人資訊。

4. 避免使用網路銀行或線上付款：使用免費 Wi-Fi 時，最好不要使用網路銀行或線上付款，以免洩露密碼等個資。

5. 不分享私人訊息：使用免費 Wi-Fi 時，盡量避免分享私人信息，例如：身分證字號、信用卡卡號。如果手機或電腦出現不正常的運作遲緩、當機或跳出警告，最好趕緊切斷 Wi-Fi，因為那可能是遭受駭客攻擊的前兆。

6. 清除紀錄並登出：使用後要記得刪除手機或電腦裡網路設定中的 Wi-Fi 存取點並登出。如果一直保持連線，駭客有可能會入侵你的個人裝置。

安心住宿篇

訪客留言、
房客投訴

 字彙出外景

🎧 12-1

① caller *n.* [C] 致電者；訪客

② message *n.* [C] 留言，訊息

③ connect sb to sb/sth *phr.* 為⋯接通⋯

④ put sb through *phr.* 為⋯接通電話

⑤ transfer *vt.* 轉（電話）

⑥ leave a message *phr.* 留下留言

⑦ take a message *phr.* 幫⋯留言

⑧ hold/hang on *phr.* 稍等一下

⑨ line *n.* [C] 電話線路

⑩ complaint *n.* [C] 抱怨，投訴

⑪ complain *vi.* 抱怨，投訴

⑫ disgusting *adj.* 令人作嘔的

⑬ annoying *adj.* 惱人的

⑭ disturbance *n.* [C][U] 干擾

⑮ leak *vi.* 漏水

⑯ apologize *vi.* 道歉

🎧 12-2

Mrs. Lopez, a caller, is speaking to a receptionist on the phone.

Receptionist: Good morning, the Holiday Inn. How may I help you?

Mrs. Lopez: I'd like to speak to Mr. Miller in Room 1607, please.

Receptionist: May I ask who is calling?

Mrs. Lopez: This is Carol Lopez.

Receptionist: Please hold on while I'm transferring your call. (*After a while*) I'm sorry. The line is busy. May I take a message?

Mrs. Lopez: Yes. Please ask him to call me on my cellphone. My number is 022-500-6600.

Receptionist: No problem. I'll make sure Mr. Miller gets the message.

致電者羅培茲女士正在跟一位飯店櫃臺接待員講電話。

接待員：早安，假日旅館。有什麼能為你服務的嗎？

羅培茲女士：我想跟 1607 號房的米勒先生通話。

接待員：請問哪裡找？

羅培茲女士：我是卡蘿‧羅培茲。

接待員：我將為你轉接電話，請稍候。(*過了一會兒*) 很抱歉。電話佔線中。要我幫你留言嗎？

羅培茲女士：好的。請他打電話到我的手機。我的電話號碼是 022-500-6600。

接待員：沒問題。我會確保米勒先生收到此訊息。

🎧 12-3

Jimmy is making a complaint to a receptionist on the phone.

Receptionist: Front desk. May I help you?

Jimmy: Yes, this is Room 643. The people in the room next to mine are too noisy! They've been playing loud music for more than half an hour. The noise is giving me a headache!

Receptionist: I'm sorry about the disturbance. We will check it immediately.

吉米正在打電話跟飯店櫃臺接待員抱怨。

接待員：這裡是櫃臺。有什麼可以幫你的嗎？

吉米：有的，這是 643 號房。我隔壁房的人太吵了！他們一直大聲地播放音樂
　　　超過半小時了。那噪音讓我頭痛！

接待員：很抱歉造成你的困擾。我們會立刻去查看。

🎧 **12-4**

Nicole is calling a receptionist to complain about the room.

Nicole: This is Room 927. I found there's water leaking from the ceiling!

Receptionist: I'm terribly sorry to hear that. I'll ask someone to go to
　　　　　　　your room and check it right away.

Nicole: Well, I'm not going to stay in this room. I want to change rooms.

Receptionist: Of course, ma'am. Let me check if there's another room
　　　　　　　available for you. (*After a while*) OK, we'll put you in
　　　　　　　Room 905 instead.

Nicole: Oh, good. Thank you.

Receptionist: My pleasure. I apologize again for the inconvenience.

妮可正在打電話跟飯店櫃臺接待員抱怨客房。

妮可：這是 927 號房。我發現天花板在漏水！

接待員：我非常抱歉聽到這個狀況。我會馬上派人去你的房間查看。

妮可：嗯，我不想繼續住這間房。我想要換房間。

接待員：當然，女士。讓我查一下還有沒有空房。(*過了一會兒*) 好的，我們會
　　　　安排 905 號房給你。

妮可：喔，太好了。謝謝你。

接待員：不客氣。再次為造成你的不便道歉。

還能這樣說

1. I'm sorry. The line is busy.

> There's no answer. 沒人接電話。
> He/She is not in right now. 他／她現在不在這裡。

2. I found there's water leaking from the ceiling!

> the ceiling is leaking 天花板在漏水
>
> my neighbors are noisy 我隔壁的房客很吵
>
> the room smells disgusting 房間聞起來很噁心
>
> my room has the smell of cigarette smoke 我的房間有菸味
>
> I can't connect to your Wi-Fi 我無法連上你們的無線網路
>
> my key card doesn't work 我的房卡不能用
>
> there is no hot water in my room 我的房間沒有熱水
>
> there is a hair in my tub and it's not mine 我的浴缸裡有頭髮而且不是我的

現在才知道

有禮貌的客訴用語 🔍

遇到問題要向飯店投訴或反應時，「禮貌」可是非常重要。
以下提供五種說法讓你表達訴求又不失禮。

1. I'm sorry to bother you, but I... 抱歉打擾你了，但是我…

   在抱怨前，先來這麼一句，這會讓整天處理抱怨的飯店職員比較樂意聆聽你的問題，並努力提供協助。

2. Can you help me with this? 可以幫我個忙嗎？

   禮貌地請求對方協助，而不要劈頭就抱怨、指責或命令對方。

3. I'm afraid there may be some misunderstanding. 恐怕其中有一些誤會。

   先委婉表示可能彼此之間有誤解，而不要怒氣沖沖地直接把過錯歸咎於對方身上。

   例如：明明當初訂的是禁菸房，但卻被安排到充滿菸味的房間時，這時可以先講
   「I'm afraid there may be some misunderstanding.」，再表明「When I made
   the room reservation, I requested a non-smoking room. 我訂房時是訂禁菸房。」

4. I understand it's not your fault, but... 我知道這不是你的錯，但…

   先給對方臺階下，化解對方的尷尬或自我防禦的心態，然後再說明問題所在。對方可能因為自知理虧而盡快解決你的問題。

5. Excuse me, but I understood that... 不好意思，但就我所了解…

   不管在飯店或其他地方，懷疑自己上當受騙時，不要和對方槓上直接說對方騙人或坑人，以免對方惱羞成怒、伺機報復。你可以間接說明自己了解的實際狀況。

   例如：Excuse me, but I understood that the taxi fare from the hotel to the
   airport was about NT$100. 不好意思，但就我所了解從飯店到機場的計程車資大概是新臺幣 100 元。

> ❗ 飯店裡總會遇到各式各樣的旅客，而其中有些人的住宿行為真的讓人受不了。知名訂房網站做了一份調查，評選出前五名惱人房客類型。讓我們一起來看看吧！
> 1. 放任小孩吵鬧的父母。
> 2. 在房間裡大吵大鬧的房客。
> 3. 在走廊上大呼小叫的房客。
> 4. 愛對飯店人員抱怨的房客。
> 5. 在飯店酒吧喝到爛醉的房客。
> 千萬不要成為令人討厭的房客喔！

安心住宿篇

延遲退房、
房間續住、
結帳退房

字彙出外景

🎧 13-1

❶ checkout time *n.* [U] 退房時間

❷ checkout date *n.* [C] 退房日期

❸ early/late checkout
　 n. [C] 提早／延遲退房

❹ early/late checkout fee
　 n. [C] 提早／延遲退房費

❺ extend *vt.* 延長，使延期

❻ move *vt.* 改變 (時間)

❼ hotel policy *n.* [C] 飯店政策

❽ turn in *phr.* 歸還，交回

❾ bill *n.* [C] 帳單

❿ settle *vi.*; *vt.* 結清，結算

⓫ expense *n.* [C][U] 費用，開銷

⓬ figure *n.* [C] 金額

⓭ charge *vt.* 收費

⓮ extra/additional charge
　 n. [C] 額外的費用

⓯ extra bed *n.* [C] 加床

⓰ swipe *vt.* 刷 (卡)

旅遊狀況句

🎧 13-2

Albert, a hotel guest, is talking to a receptionist on the phone.

Albert: Hello, this is Room 443. I'd like to request a late checkout.

Receptionist: We aren't fully booked now, so it's not a problem. You can keep your room until 2:00 p.m. Is that OK?

Albert: That really helps. Thanks.

飯店房客亞伯特正在和一位飯店櫃臺接待員講電話。

亞伯特：你好，這是 443 號房。我想要求延後退房。

接待員：我們目前房間還沒有被預訂滿，所以沒問題。你的房間可以保留到下午兩點。可以嗎？

亞伯特：真是幫了大忙。謝謝。

🎧 13-3

Olivia, a hotel guest, is talking to a receptionist on the phone.

Olivia: Hi, this is Olivia Evans in Room 983. I need to stay in town for two more days. Can I extend my reservation? I'd like to move my checkout date to March 6th.

Receptionist: Let me check. (*After a while*) OK, that can be arranged. There is a single room available for two nights. You will have to pay an extra charge of $250 for two more nights. Is that OK?

Olivia: No problem.

飯店房客奧莉維亞正在和一位飯店櫃臺接待員講電話。

奧莉維亞：嗨，我是住在 983 號房的奧莉維亞・艾文思。我需要在城裡多待兩天。我可以延長住宿嗎？我想把退房日期改到三月六日。

接待員：讓我查一下。(過了一會兒) 沒問題，可以安排。還有一間單人空房可以住兩晚。你多住兩晚會需要多付 250 美元的額外費用。可以嗎？

奧莉維亞：沒問題。

安心住宿篇—延遲退房、房間續住、結帳退房

Perry, a hotel guest, is checking out at the front desk.

Perry: Hello. I'd like to check out. Here's my key card.

Receptionist: OK. Did you use the minibar in your room?

Perry: No.

Receptionist: OK. Sir, let's check your bill. Additional charges include the room service and an extra bed. Is that correct?

Perry: Yes. That's correct.

Receptionist: How would you like to pay, sir?

Perry: I'd like to pay by credit card.

Receptionist: (*Swiping the card*) Would you sign here, please?

Perry: Sure. (*Signing the receipt*)

Receptionist: Thank you, sir. We look forward to seeing you again.

飯店房客派瑞正在飯店櫃臺辦理退房手續。

派瑞：你好，我想辦理退房手續。這是我的房卡。

接待員：好的。你有使用過房間內的迷你吧嗎？

派瑞：沒有。

接待員：好的。先生，我們一起確認你的帳單。額外費用包括客房餐飲服務和加床費。對嗎？

派瑞：是的。沒錯。

接待員：你要如何付款，先生？

派瑞：我想要用信用卡付款。

接待員：(*刷卡*) 可以請你在這裡簽名嗎？

派瑞：當然可以。(*在收據上簽名*)

接待員：謝謝你，先生。我們期待再與你相見。

還能這樣說

1. Did you **use the minibar** in your room?

> <u>have/take</u> anything from the minibar 吃／拿迷你吧的任何東西
> order anything from room service 和客房餐飲服務點了任何東西
> make any <u>local/domestic/international</u> calls 撥打本地／國內／國際電話

 本地電話通常是指在同一縣、市或州內的電話。
國內電話則通常指在非同一縣、市或州的國內電話。

2. We **look forward to** seeing you again.

> hope you have a safe trip back home 希望你平安到家
> hope you enjoyed your stay with us 希望你住得滿意
> hope we'll have the chance to serve you again 希望有機會再為你服務

現在才知道

飯店的額外收費 🔍

除了住宿費之外,你知道飯店其實還有其他需要額外付費的服務嗎?

一起來看看有哪些可能的費用吧!

1. 取消訂房:若要取消訂房,大多數的飯店規定必須在入住前四十八小時或七十二小時前取消預訂。若超過取消時間,飯店可能會收取部分費用作為補償。

> ❗ 因為預訂時就需提供信用卡資料作為訂房擔保,所以即便沒有入住,飯店還是可以依據此資料扣款。所以在訂房時,要特別留意訂房相關規定。

2. 提前入住:一般飯店的入住時間是下午三點後,如果想提早入住,就可能得支付額外費用。

> ❗ 不過多數飯店都有提供免費的行李寄存服務,若不想拎著大包小包旅行,也可以先到飯店寄放行李喔!等當日行程結束回飯店時再辦理入住手續。

3. 迷你吧:迷你吧的零食或飲料可能要收費喔!通常迷你吧食物的定價比市價高,使用前一定要確認是否需付費,以免荷包大失血。若旁邊有標示 free (免費的)、complimentary (免費贈送的) 或 with compliments (免費贈送),就表示是飯店招待的迎賓點心。如果還是不確定,也可以撥電話到櫃臺詢問喔。

迷你吧要確認是否需付費喔!

茶包和咖啡通常是免費提供。

4. 隨選電影 (Movies on Demand):有些飯店的電視節目需要收費喔!看到院線電影時,別高興得太早,因為通常要另外付費才能繼續收看。如果有小孩或不諳外語的旅伴,建議把遙控器收好,以免誤觸產生額外費用。

5. 客房餐飲服務：會將餐點送至客房內，從早餐到宵夜一應俱全，但是價格通常比外面餐廳高。一般也需要給服務人員餐費的10%到15%作為小費。

6. 提前退房費：入住後，若因行程規畫而需要減少入住天數並提早退房的話，有可能會被酌收手續費或是不退費但提供住宿券供下次使用。

7. 延遲退房費：一般飯店的退房時間為上午十一點或十二點，如果超過時間退房，就可能會被加收費用。但多數飯店在有空房的情況下，會提供免費延遲退房。而有些飯店也會為飯店會員、入住行政套房等房客免費延遲退房。

8. 其他：依據各家飯店規定不同，可能酌收的費用還有飯店接駁費、停車費、行李搬運費及健身房使用費等。

＊對帳單有疑問時，你可以這樣說：

(1) Excuse me, what's this charge? 不好意思，這筆費用是？

(2) I don't know what this charge is for. 我不知道這是支付什麼的費用。

(3) I'm afraid there's a mistake on my bill. 恐怕我的帳單內容有誤。

美食當前篇

餐廳預約

 字彙出外景

 14-1

1. breakfast/brunch/lunch/dinner reservation *n.* [C] 早餐／早午餐／午餐／晚餐訂位

2. take/accept a reservation *phr.* 接受訂位

3. hold a reservation for sth *phr.* 保留…(時間) 的訂位

4. modify/postpone a reservation *phr.* 修改／延後訂位

5. reservation code *n.* [C] 預約代號

6. party *n.* [C] 一群人

7. table for sth *phr.* …(人數) 的位子

8. be fully booked (up) *phr.* 被訂滿

9. non-smoking section *n.* [C] 禁菸區

10. parking lot *n.* [C] 停車場

11. parking space *n.* [C] 停車位

12. dine *vi.* 用餐

13. come by *phr.* 到訪，造訪

14. dress code *n.* [C] 服裝規定

15. dining time limit *n.* [C] 用餐時間限制

16. minimum charge *n.* [C] 最低消費

17. service charge *n.* [C] 服務費

18. corkage fee *n.* [C] 開瓶費

🎧 14-2

Carol is calling Jimmy Kitchen to make a dinner reservation.

Clerk: Jimmy Kitchen. How may I help you?

Carol: I'd like to reserve a table for tonight at 7:00 p.m.

Clerk: How many people will be in your party?

Carol: Three.

Clerk: Could I have your name and phone number, please?

Carol: It's Carol Lopez. C-A-R-O-L L-O-P-E-Z. And my cellphone number is 022-500-6600.

Clerk: Alright, Ms. Lopez. I have reserved a table under your name for three at 7:00 p.m.

Carol: Great. Thanks.

卡蘿正在打電話到吉米廚房為晚餐訂位。

店員：吉米廚房。有什麼能為你服務的嗎？

卡蘿：我想要預訂今晚七點的位子。

店員：你們總共有幾位？

卡蘿：三位。

店員：可以給我你的名字和電話號碼嗎？

卡蘿：卡蘿‧羅培茲。C-A-R-O-L L-O-P-E-Z。我的手機號碼是 022-500-6600。

店員：好的，羅培茲小姐。我已經以你的名字預訂了晚上七點鐘三個人的位子。

卡蘿：太好了。謝謝。

14-3

Sandra is calling Tasty Restaurant to make a lunch reservation.

Sandra: Hello, I'd like to make a lunch reservation for this Wednesday.

Clerk: How many are you?

Sandra: Four. And please give me a table in the non-smoking section.

Clerk: No problem. What time will you be here?

Sandra: About 12:30 p.m. By the way, is there any parking lot near your restaurant?

Clerk: Yes, there is one across from our restaurant. You can park your car there.

珊卓拉正在打電話到美味餐廳為午餐訂位。

珊卓拉：你好，我想要預訂這個星期三午餐的位子。

店員：你們有幾位呢？

珊卓拉：四位。請給我禁菸區的位子。

店員：沒問題。你們幾點會到呢？

珊卓拉：大約十二點半。順帶一提，你們餐廳附近有停車場嗎？

店員：有的，我們餐廳對面有一個停車場。你可以將車子停在那裡。

14-4

Ethan is calling Pluto Restaurant to make a dinner reservation.

Ethan: Hi, I'd like to make a reservation for dinner on December 20th.

Clerk: OK. When would you like to dine, and what name will the reservation be under?

Ethan: We'd like to come by at 7:30 p.m., and the reservation will be under Ethan Scott.

Clerk: I'm sorry there aren't any tables left for 7:30 p.m., but we can give you one at 8:30 p.m.

Ethan: That will be fine.

伊森正在打電話到布魯托餐廳為晚餐訂位。

伊森：嗨，我想要預訂十二月二十日的晚餐座位。

店員：好的。你要幾點來用餐和用哪個名字訂位？

伊森：我們想七點半到，訂位人是伊森·史考特。

店員：很抱歉晚上七點半沒有空位了，但我們八點半有位子。

伊森：可以。

還能這樣說

1. Please give me a table in the non-smoking section.

a table in the smoking section 吸菸區的位子

a table by the window 靠窗的位子

a table with a view 有景觀的位子

a table on the balcony 觀景臺上的位子

a table away from the kitchen 遠離廚房的位子

a private dining room 私人用餐包廂

2. I'm sorry there aren't any tables left for 7:30 p.m.

all the tables are reserved until 8:30 p.m. 八點半才有空位

we don't take reservations for lunch/dinner 我們午餐／晚餐不接受預訂

we don't take reservations on weekends 我們週末不接受預訂

we are fully booked up/have no tables available 我們已經客滿了

現在才知道

訂位的技巧

1. 透過網路或手機 app 預訂餐廳。你就能輕輕鬆鬆訂到熱門的餐廳，還能瀏覽菜單、餐點照片或餐廳評價，避免踩到地雷。

2. 信用卡福利多！有些銀行提供祕書服務，協助語言不通的你預訂餐廳、機票等。快看看你的信用卡有沒有此服務吧！

3. 行程確定後，就盡早訂位。餐廳通常希望顧客能提早半個月到一個月前訂位。因為他們會保留部分座位給現場的客人，來提高翻桌率。

4. 用餐的高峰時段是中午十二點到一點半和晚上五點半到七點半。因此避開這兩個黃金時段，比較容易訂到位子。

＊訂位時可能會想問：

   (1) Does your restaurant have a dress code? 請問你們餐廳有服裝規定嗎？

   (2) Do you have a dining time limit? 請問你們有用餐時間限制嗎？

   (3) Do you have a minimum charge? 請問你們有最低消費嗎？

   (4) Do you add a service charge? 請問你們有加服務費嗎？

   (5) Will there be a corkage fee? 請問需要開瓶費嗎？

美食當前篇

Unit 15

現場候位、
帶領入座

字彙出外景

🎧 15-1

1. headwaiter *n.* [C] 領班

2. host/hostess *n.* [C] (男／女) 領檯

3. host station *n.* [C] (餐廳) 接待櫃臺

4. take sb's name *phr.* 記下…的名字

5. wait/waiting list *n.* [C] 等候名單

6. wait/waiting time *n.* [U] 等候時間

7. waiting area *n.* [C] 候位區

8. notify *vt.* 通知，告知

9. terrace *n.* [C] 露臺

10. main dining room *n.* [C] 主要用餐區

11. indoor/outdoor seat
    n. [C] 室內／戶外座位

12. booth/bar seat
    n. [C] 沙發雅座／吧檯座位

13. seating *n.* [U] 座位數

14. accessible seating *n.* [U] 無障礙座位

15. share *vi.*; *vt.* 合用，共用

16. free/reserved table
    n. [C] 空著的／已被預訂的桌子

旅遊狀況句

15-2

Alan is talking with a headwaiter at the host station.

Headwaiter: Welcome to Merlin Restaurant. Do you have a reservation?

Alan: No, we don't.

Headwaiter: I'm afraid there aren't any tables available at the moment. Would you like me to put your name on the waiting list?

Alan: OK. Thanks.

Headwaiter: Could I have your name, please?

Alan: Alan Marshall.

Headwaiter: How many people are there in your party?

Alan: Three.

Headwaiter: OK. I'll notify you when the table is ready.

(After fifteen minutes)

Headwaiter: Mr. Marshall, party of three. Please come to the host station.

Alan: Is our table ready?

Headwaiter: Yes. Let me take you to your table.

艾倫正在接待櫃臺和一位領班談話。

領班：歡迎光臨梅林餐廳。你們有訂位嗎？

艾倫：我們沒有。

領班：目前恐怕沒有空位。你要我將你的名字放在等候名單上嗎？

艾倫：好的。謝謝。

領班：請問你的名字是？

艾倫：艾倫‧馬歇爾。

領班：請問你們有幾位呢？

艾倫：三位。

領班：好的。你們的桌子準備好時，我會告知你。

(十五分鐘後)

領班：三位的馬歇爾先生。請至接待櫃臺。

艾倫：我們的桌子準備好了嗎？

領班：是的。容我為你們帶位。

🎧 15-3

Stephanie is talking with a headwaiter in a restaurant.

Stephanie: Hi, we'd like a table for four, please.

Headwaiter: I'm sorry, but all our tables are taken now.

Stephanie: We have to attend a conference in about an hour. How long will we have to wait?

Headwaiter: At least thirty minutes. Would you like to wait?

Stephanie: No, thanks. Maybe next time.

Headwaiter: We apologize for the inconvenience.

史蒂芬妮正在餐廳和一位領班談話。

史蒂芬妮：嗨，請給我們四個人的位子。

領班：很抱歉，現在客滿了。

史蒂芬妮：我們大概一小時後要參加會議。要等多久呢？

領班：至少三十分鐘。你們要等位子嗎？

史蒂芬妮：不了，謝謝。下次有機會的話。

領班：我們很抱歉造成你的不便。

🎧 15-4

Antonio is talking with a headwaiter in a Mexican restaurant.

Headwaiter: Good evening, sir.

Antonio: Good evening. Do you have any booth seats available?

Headwaiter: Unfortunately, we don't. Would you mind sitting at the bar? If you are OK with bar seats, I can seat you right away.

Antonio: Well, I don't mind.

Headwaiter: OK. Follow me, please.

安東尼奧正在墨西哥餐廳和一位領班談話。

領班：晚安，先生。

安東尼奧：晚安。你們還有沙發雅座嗎？

領班：很不湊巧地，沒有了。你介意坐吧檯嗎？如果你願意坐吧檯座位，我可以馬上為你安排。

安東尼奧：嗯，我不介意。

領班：好的。請跟我來。

還能這樣說

1. No, thanks. Maybe next time.

We'd rather not wait. 我們還是不等了。
We'll come another time. 我們改天再來。

2. Would you mind sitting at the bar?

sharing a table 併桌
sitting separately 分開坐
waiting until one is free 等到有空位
waiting for about thirty minutes 等候大約三十分鐘

3. If you are OK with bar seats, I can seat you right away.

I might be able to seat you sooner if you're OK with booth seats.
如果你願意坐沙發雅座，我能更早讓你入座。
If you're not in the waiting area when we call your name, we'll give your table away. 如果叫到你的名字時，你沒有在等候區，我們將會讓出你的座位。

現在才知道

候位禮儀大不同 🔍

各國風俗民情不同，候位當然也有要注意的禮節，以免誤踩地雷，成為奧客喔！

1. 進入國外餐廳，不論是高級或平價餐廳、客人多寡(除了速食店或櫃臺點餐後立即付錢的咖啡廳)，都要在接待櫃臺等候領班安排座位。千萬不要看到空位，就自行入座。

 特別注意：就算親友已經入座，通常還是需由領班帶領入座，而非自行進入餐廳找人喔。

2. 領班見到候位客人時通常會詢問：「How are you today? 你今天過得如何？」這時可以回答：「Good, thanks. 很不錯，謝謝。」不需要長篇大論報告自己的情況，這只是客套的問候開場白。

3. 講完問候語後，領班會詢問用餐人數或想要什麼樣的位子。對座位的要求都可以在此時提出(請見 Unit 14)，領班會盡量安排。若入座後有問題也可以和服務人員反應，千萬不要自己亂換位子。

4. 若對座位有其他要求，例如：想要坐窗邊、禁菸區等，可能就需要花比較多時間等待上一組客人離開。反之，若對座位沒有特別的要求，也可以接受和同行友人分開入座，通常可以大幅縮減候位時間喔！

美食當前篇

瀏覽菜單、
選擇餐點

 字彙出外景

🎧 16-1

① server *n.* [C] 服務生

② waiter/waitress *n.* [C] (男／女) 服務生

③ menu *n.* [C] 菜單

④ take sb's time *phr.* …慢慢來

⑤ take sb's order *phr.* 幫…點菜

⑥ starter/appetizer *n.* [C] 前菜，開胃菜

⑦ cocktail *n.* [C] 雞尾酒

⑧ aperitif *n.* [C] 開胃酒

⑨ entrée/main course *n.* [C] 主餐

⑩ side dish/order *n.* [C] 附餐

⑪ signature dish *n.* [C] 招牌菜

⑫ special *n.* [C] 特餐

⑬ business set *n.* [C] 商業套餐

⑭ combo/combination meal *n.* [C] 套餐

⑮ care for *phr.* 想要

⑯ dessert *n.* [C][U] 甜點

⑰ wine list *n.* [C] 酒單

旅遊狀況句

16-2

Claude is talking with a server in a restaurant.

Server: Good evening, sir. Here's the menu. Please take your time.

Claude: Thank you.

(*After a few minutes*)

Server: May I take your order?

Claude: I think I'd like a little more time.

Server: Sure. I'll come back in a little while.

克勞德正在餐廳和一位服務生談話。

服務生：晚安，先生。這裡是菜單。請你慢慢看。

克勞德：謝謝。

(幾分鐘後)

服務生：要幫你點餐了嗎？

克勞德：我想我還需要一些時間。

服務生：好的。我一會兒再回來。

16-3

Hanna is talking with a server in a restaurant.

Server: Good afternoon, ma'am. Are you ready to order now?

Hanna: Yes, I am.

Server: Could I get you something to start with?

Hanna: Sure. I'd like a martini as an aperitif.

Server: Certainly. Would you like to have a salad?

Hanna: Yes, a mixed salad would be nice.

Server: What kind of dressing would you like to have on your salad? French, Thousand Island, Caesar, or oil and vinegar?

Hanna: Oil and vinegar, please.

Server: Good choice. What would you like for your main course?

Hanna: I'll try the grilled lamb chops.

Server: OK. Would you care for dessert?

Hanna: I'd like apple pie.

Server: Sure, and would you like to have some wine?

Hanna: A glass of red wine, please.

Server: No problem. Let me repeat your order. You'd like a martini, a mixed salad with oil and vinegar dressing, the grilled lamb chops, apple pie and a glass of red wine. Would you like anything else, ma'am?

Hanna: That's all. Thank you.

Server: OK. I'll be back with your order soon.

漢娜正在餐廳和一位服務生談話。

服務生：午安，女士。你現在準備好要點餐了嗎？

漢娜：是的。

服務生：你要先來點什麼嗎？

漢娜：當然。我想要一杯馬丁尼當餐前酒。

服務生：沒問題。你想要來份沙拉嗎？

漢娜：要，一份綜合沙拉就很不錯。

服務生：你的沙拉要搭配哪種醬汁？法式、千島、凱薩或油醋醬？

漢娜：請給我油醋醬。

服務生：很棒的選擇。那你的主餐要點什麼呢？

漢娜：我要試試烤羊排。

服務生：好的。你想要甜點嗎？

漢娜：我想要蘋果派。

服務生：沒問題，你要點些酒嗎？

漢娜：請給我一杯紅酒。

服務生：沒問題。讓我重複你的餐點。你要一杯馬丁尼、一份綜合沙拉佐油醋醬、烤羊排、蘋果派和一杯紅酒。你還要點什麼嗎，女士？

漢娜：就這些。謝謝。

服務生：好的。我很快會回來為你上菜。

還能這樣說

1. I'd like a martini as an aperitif.

> try roast chicken 試試烤雞
>
> take today's special 點今日特餐
>
> like to order sirloin steak 想點沙朗牛排
>
> have the fried chicken with a baked potato 要炸雞配烤馬鈴薯
>
> have a soufflé for dessert 我的甜點要舒芙蕾

2. Would you care for dessert?

> like a starter/appetizer 要前菜嗎
>
> like something to eat 要吃些什麼
>
> like anything to drink 要喝點什麼
>
> like to see the wine list 要看看酒單嗎
>
> like to have a cup of coffee 要來杯咖啡嗎
>
> like to try our soup of the day 要試試我們的本日湯品嗎

現在才知道

英文菜單大解密 🔍

想到在國外餐廳點餐就頭皮發麻嗎？不要緊張，快看下列菜單上常出現的菜色，讓你出國照樣可以順利點餐、享受美食。

前菜 (starter/appetizer)	雞翅 (chicken wing) 起司條 (mozzarella stick) 培根香腸捲 (pigs in a blanket) 肉丸 (meatball)	洋蔥圈 (onion ring) 燻鮭魚 (smoked salmon) 鵝肝 (foie gras) 扇貝 (scallop)
湯 (soup)	蛤蜊巧達湯 (clam chowder) 洋蔥湯 (onion soup) 龍蝦法式濃湯 (lobster bisque)	羅宋湯 (borscht) 蘑菇濃湯 (mushroom soup)
沙拉 (salad)	綜合沙拉 (mixed salad) 田園沙拉 (garden salad)	主廚沙拉 (chef salad) 水果沙拉 (fruit salad)
主餐 (main course)	海陸雙拼 (surf and turf) 豬肋排 (baby back ribs) 雞胸肉 (chicken breast) 羊排 (lamb chop) 魚排 (fish filet)	沙朗牛排 (sirloin steak) 菲力牛排 (filet mignon) 肋眼牛排 (ribeye steak) 丁骨牛排 (T-bone steak)
	熟度 一分熟 (rare) 三分熟 (medium-rare) 五分熟 (medium)	七分熟 (medium-well) 全熟 (well-done)
三明治 (sandwich)	烤牛肉三明治 (roast beef sandwich) 火雞肉三明治 (turkey sandwich) 雞肉三明治 (chicken sandwich) 總匯三明治 (club sandwich) 蔬菜三明治 (veggie sandwich)	

麵包 (bread)	白麵包 (white bread) 全麥麵包 (whole wheat bread)	黑麥麵包 (rye bread) 雜糧麵包 (multigrain bread)
配餐 (side dish)	薯條 (French fries) 馬鈴薯泥 (mashed potatoes)	薯餅 (hash browns)
漢堡配料 (hamburger topping)	甜椒 (sweet pepper) 黑橄欖 (olive) 小黃瓜 (cucumber)	洋蔥 (onion) 醃黃瓜 (pickle)

> ❗ 如果吃素也可以點素漢堡 (veggie burger) 喔！

義大利麵食 (pasta)	細長圓柱麵 (spaghetti) 筆管麵 (penne) 細扁麵 (linguini) 寬扁麵 (fettuccine)	千層麵 (lasagna) 螺旋麵 (rotini/fusilli) 貝殼麵 (conchiglie) 義式餃子 (ravioli)
	醬汁 青醬 (pesto/green sauce) 番茄紅醬 (marinara/tomato sauce) 奶油白醬 (alfredo/cream sauce) 番茄肉醬 (bolognese sauce)	
甜點 (dessert)	起司蛋糕 (cheesecake) 布朗尼蛋糕 (brownie) 提拉米蘇 (tiramisu)	奶酪 (panna cotta) 派 (pie) 塔 (tart)
飲料 (beverage)	茶 (tea) 花草茶 (herbal tea) 咖啡 (coffee) 果汁 (juice)	可樂 (Coke) 汽水 (soda pop) 檸檬水 (lemonade) 奶昔 (smoothie)

美食當前篇

餐點成分、
餐點推薦、
餐點客製

字彙出外景

🎧 17-1

❶ chef's special *n.* [C] 主廚特餐

❷ homemade *adj.* 自製的

❸ sauce *n.* [U] 醬，調味汁

❹ ingredient *n.* [C] 成分，材料

❺ dairy product *n.* [C] 乳製品

❻ be allergic/have an allergy to sth

　phr. 對⋯過敏

❼ portion/serving

　n. [C] (食物) 一份，一客

❽ prepare *vt.* 烹調

❾ recommend *vt.* 推薦

❿ be in the mood for sth *phr.* 想要⋯

⓫ go with sth *phr.* 與⋯搭配

⓬ steam *vt.* 蒸

⓭ sauté *vt.* 嫩煎，拌炒

⓮ stir-fry *vi.*; *vt.* 快炒

⓯ pan-fry *vt.* 煎

⓰ deep-fry *vt.* 炸

⓱ simmer/stew *vt.* 燉

⓲ boil *vt.* 汆燙

⓳ bake *vi.*; *vt.* 烘焙

⓴ upsize *vt.* 加大

 旅遊狀況句

🎧 17-2

Melody is talking with a server in a restaurant.

Melody: What's the chef's special today?

Server: It's pork chops with homemade plum sauce.

Melody: How is the pork prepared?

Server: It's first pan-fried and then stewed.

Melody: How big is a portion?

Server: It's enough for two people.

Melody: Well, it will be too much for me. I think I'll have spaghetti and meatballs. Could I get my order without garlic?

Server: No problem, ma'am.

美樂蒂正在餐廳和一位服務生談話。

美樂蒂：今天的主廚特餐是什麼？

服務生：是豬排配自製梅子醬。

美樂蒂：這豬肉是怎麼烹調的？

服務生：先煎過再燉煮。

美樂蒂：一份有多大？

服務生：足夠兩個人吃。

美樂蒂：嗯，對我而言太多了。我想我要一份肉丸義大利麵。我的餐點裡可以不加大蒜嗎？

服務生：沒問題，女士。

🎧 17-3

Matthew is talking with a server in a restaurant.

Matthew: I'm not sure what to order. Do you offer any low-calorie dishes? What do you recommend?

Server: I'd recommend our garlic baked salmon. It is very tasty.

Matthew: I am not in the mood for fish tonight.

Server: Would you like to try the sautéed chicken breast? It's also very good.

Matthew: Great. I'll take that.

Server: Would you like to order some wine with your meal?

Matthew: Sure. What would you suggest?

Server: I'd recommend our Chardonnay. It goes very well with the chicken breast.

馬修正在餐廳和一位服務生談話。

馬修：我不確定要點什麼。你們有提供低卡路里餐點嗎？你推薦什麼？

服務生：我推薦我們的蒜香烤鮭魚。非常美味。

馬修：我今晚不想吃魚。

服務生：那要試試嫩煎雞胸肉嗎？它也很棒。

馬修：太好了。我要點那個。

服務生：你要點些酒搭配你的餐嗎？

馬修：當然。你建議點什麼？

服務生：我會推薦我們的夏多內白酒。它跟雞胸肉很搭。

17-4

Nicole is ordering a meal in a fast food restaurant.

Server: Welcome to Yummy Burger. What would you like to order?

Nicole: I'll have a cheeseburger combo meal. No pickle, please. I'm allergic to pickles.

Server: OK. Would you like to upsize your meal for eighty cents more? You'll get a large Coke and a large French fries.

Nicole: No, thanks. Oh, could I get a smoothie with that, instead of a soda pop?

Server: Sure, but it'll cost an extra $1. For here or to go?

Nicole: No problem. To go, thank you.

妮可正在一家速食餐廳點餐。

服務生：歡迎光臨美味漢堡。你想要點什麼？

妮可：我要一份起司漢堡套餐。不要酸黃瓜。我對酸黃瓜過敏。

服務生：好的。你要多加 80 分加大套餐嗎？你會有一杯大可樂和一份大薯條。

妮可：不了，謝謝。喔，我可以搭配奶昔，不要汽水嗎？

服務生：當然可以，但是要多加 1 美元。內用還是外帶？

妮可：沒問題。外帶，謝謝。

還能這樣說

1. Could I get my order without garlic?

chili 辣椒	celery 芹菜	cilantro 香菜
onion 洋蔥	ginger 薑	parsley 香芹 (洋香菜)
scallion/green onion 蔥	(black) pepper (黑) 胡椒	sweet pepper 甜椒

2. Do you offer any low-calorie dishes?

child meals 兒童餐點	lactose-free meals 無乳糖餐點
halal options 清真餐點	gluten-free meals 無麩質餐點
vegetarian meals 素食餐點	

3. I'm allergic to pickles.

shellfish 貝類、甲殼類	milk 牛奶	wheat 小麥
oysters 牡蠣	honey 蜂蜜	peanuts 花生
crabs 螃蟹	kiwis 奇異果	almonds 杏仁
seafood 海鮮	gluten 麩質	sesame 芝麻

現在才知道

點餐小祕訣 🔍

在國外點菜時，如果看不懂外文菜單或有選擇困難，你可以請服務生推薦餐廳的當季餐點 (seasonal meal)、最受歡迎的菜餚 (the most popular dish)、暢銷餐點 (best seller) 或招牌菜 (the specialty of the house) 等。此外，也可以先跟服務生溝通你的飲食偏好，例如：不能吃辣等，以免選到不適合自己口味的菜餚。

對特定食物過敏的人，若遇到不認識的菜名或怕吃到讓自己過敏的食材，一定要先詢問服務生關於餐點的成分或主動告知自己對哪些食物過敏喔！當然也有部分餐廳會在菜單上標示過敏原。有些餐廳甚至會規劃無敏料理區，廚師會用專門的刀具、砧板在特定的工作區烹煮，以免汙染食物。上菜時也會標示為無敏餐點，讓顧客安心食用。

有些店家會貼心地在菜單上以圖片標示餐點含有哪些食材喔！

美食當前篇

催促餐點、
送餐錯誤、
要求餐具、
打包餐點

 字彙出外景

🎧 18-1

① serve *vt.* 提供 (飲食)

② chef *n.* [C] 主廚

③ fork *n.* [C] 叉子

④ spoon *n.* [C] 湯匙

⑤ knife *n.* [C] 刀

⑥ plate *n.* [C] 盤子

⑦ chipped *adj.* 有缺口的，破損的

⑧ napkin *n.* [C] 餐巾 (紙)

⑨ smoke *vi.*; *vt.* 抽菸

⑩ ashtray *n.* [C] 菸灰缸

⑪ wine glass *n.* [C] 酒杯

⑫ saucer *n.* [C] 茶碟

⑬ refill *vt.* 再添滿；*n.* [C] 再添滿

⑭ leftovers *n.* (*pl.*) 剩飯剩菜

⑮ full *adj.* 吃飽的

⑯ pack/wrap up *phr.* 打包

⑰ get sth to go *phr.* 打包⋯

⑱ doggy bag *n.* [C] 打包袋

⑲ takeout box *n.* [C] 外帶餐盒

🎧 18-2

Gloria is talking with a server in a restaurant.

Server: What can I do for you?

Gloria: I wonder why my steak is taking so long.

Server: I'm sorry, ma'am. I'll check your order right away.

Gloria: Could you serve my meal quickly, please? I ordered my meal fifty minutes ago, and it still hasn't come.

葛羅莉亞正在餐廳和一位服務生談話。

服務生：有什麼可以幫你的嗎？

葛羅莉亞：我想知道為什麼我的牛排要這麼久。

服務生：抱歉，女士。我立刻去確認你的餐點。

葛羅莉亞：可以請你快點幫我上菜嗎？我五十分鐘前點了餐，到現在都還沒來。

🎧 18-3

Harold is talking with a server in a restaurant.

Server: Your steak, sir.

Harold: This is not what I ordered.

Server: I'm sorry, sir. What was your order?

Harold: I ordered a beef sandwich and onion rings.

Server: I'm very sorry for the mistake. I'll check your order with our chef.

哈洛德正在餐廳和一位服務生談話。

服務生：你的牛排，先生。

哈洛德：這不是我點的。

服務生：抱歉，先生。你點的是什麼？

哈洛德：我點的是牛肉三明治和洋蔥圈。

服務生：很抱歉弄錯了。我會和我們的主廚核對你的餐點。

美食當前篇｜催促餐點、送餐錯誤、要求餐具、打包餐點

 18-4

Rosa is talking with a server in a restaurant.

Rosa: Excuse me. I dropped my fork on the floor, and I found my plate is chipped. May I have new ones?

Server: Certainly, ma'am. I'll bring you new ones right away.

Rosa: Thank you. Could you also bring me an ashtray? I'd like to smoke.

Server: I'm sorry, ma'am. All restaurants in the city are non-smoking.

Rosa: Oh, I see. That's OK.

羅莎正在餐廳和一位服務生談話。

羅莎：不好意思。我的叉子掉到地上了，還有我發現我的盤子有缺口。我可以要新的嗎？

服務生：當然可以，女士。我馬上拿新的給你。

羅莎：謝謝。你可以也拿一個菸灰缸給我嗎？我想要抽菸。

服務生：抱歉，女士。本市所有餐廳都禁止吸菸。

羅莎：喔，我了解了。沒關係。

 18-5

Derek is talking with a server in a restaurant.

Server: May I clear your table?

Derek: Sure, we're all done. We are too full to finish the sandwich. Could I get this to go?

Server: Of course. I'll put it in a doggy bag for you.

德瑞克正在餐廳和一位服務生談話。

服務生：可以清理你的桌面嗎？

德瑞克：當然可以，我們吃完了。我們吃不完這個三明治。我可以打包這個嗎？

服務生：當然可以。我會幫你把它放進打包袋。

還能這樣說

1. I found **my plate is chipped**.

> this glass cracked 這個玻璃杯裂掉了
>
> there's a lipstick stain on this glass 這個玻璃杯上有口紅印
>
> this <u>spoon/fork/knife/plate</u> is dirty 這個<u>湯匙／叉子／刀子／盤子</u>有髒汙

2. **Could I get this to go?**

> Could I <u>bring/take</u> this home? 我能帶這個回家嗎？
>
> Could I have a doggy bag for my sandwich? 我能要一個打包袋裝三明治嗎？
>
> Could you give me a takeout box? 你能給我一個外帶餐盒嗎？
>
> Could you wrap up the leftovers for us? 你能幫我們打包剩飯剩菜嗎？

現在才知道

西餐相關小知識 🔍

☆ **西餐餐具的擺放位置**

　　想到要在西式餐廳用餐，面對琳瑯滿目的刀叉、杯盤碟子，就頭昏眼花嗎？害怕用錯餐具而出糗嗎？別怕，下面為你整理西餐餐具的擺放位置。

① 沙拉叉 (salad fork)	⑨ 座位牌 (place card)	⑰ 海鮮叉 (seafood fork)
② 魚叉 (fish fork)	⑩ 沙拉盤 (salad plate)	⑱ 水杯 (water goblet)
③ 主餐叉 (dinner fork)	⑪ 湯碗 (soup bowl)	⑲ 香檳杯
④ 餐巾(紙) (napkin)	⑫ 主餐盤 (service plate)	(champagne flute)
⑤ 奶油刀 (butter knife)	⑬ 主餐刀 (meal knife)	⑳ 紅酒杯
⑥ 麵包盤 (bread plate)	⑭ 魚刀 (fish knife)	(red wine glass)
⑦ 點心匙 (dessert spoon)	⑮ 茶匙 (teaspoon)	㉑ 白酒杯
⑧ 點心叉 (dessert fork)	⑯ 湯匙 (soup spoon)	(white wine glass)

☆ 使用小知識

1. 餐巾通常會擺放在餐盤上或在餐盤左側。請將餐巾放在大腿上,不要當圍兜使用喔。有時服務生也會幫客人鋪餐巾。

2. 餐具的使用原則:以餐盤為中心,由外側使用至內側。

3. 不要在餐盤上磨出聲音,也不要先把主餐全部切成塊狀再食用,這樣很不禮貌。

4. 酒杯的差異:香檳杯為細長型,除了可以避免氣泡過快消散外,也可以欣賞氣泡在杯內流動的美感;而紅酒杯較白酒杯大,如此一來紅酒與空氣接觸的面積比較多,就比較容易醒酒。

☆ 刀叉擺放傳遞的訊息

你知道刀叉的擺放位置也有學問嗎?快來認識吧!

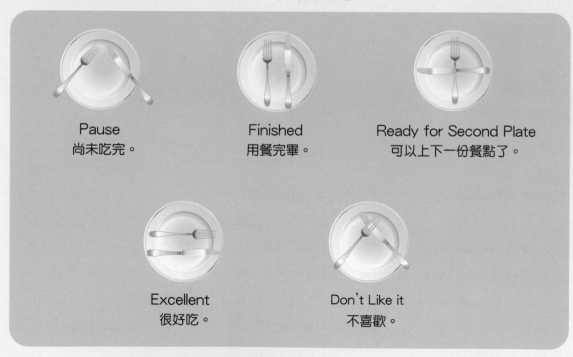

Pause
尚未吃完。

Finished
用餐完畢。

Ready for Second Plate
可以上下一份餐點了。

Excellent
很好吃。

Don't Like it
不喜歡。

美食當前篇

餐廳抱怨

 字彙出外景

🎧 **19-1**

① on the house *phr.* 店家免費招待的

② overcook *vt.* 把…煮得太熟

③ undercook *vt.* 沒把…煮熟

④ raw *adj.* 生的

⑤ stale *adj.* 不新鮮的

⑥ mushy *adj.* 糊爛的

⑦ chewy *adj.* 難嚼的

⑧ tough *adj.* 老的，不易切開的

⑨ sour *adj.* 酸的

⑩ sweet *adj.* 甜的

⑪ salty *adj.* 鹹的

⑫ bitter *adj.* 苦的

⑬ spicy *adj.* 辣的

⑭ take sth away *phr.* 拿走…

⑮ stain *vt.* 弄髒；*n.* [C] 汙漬

⑯ assure *vt.* 向…保證

⑰ lower *vt.* 降低，減少

⑱ compensate *vt.* 賠償，補償

⑲ apology *n.* [C] 道歉

🎧 **19-2**

Willie is making a complaint to a server in a restaurant.

Server: Yes, sir. How may I help you?

Willie: I think there's a hair in my soup.

Server: I'm terribly sorry about that, sir. I'll bring you another one right away. It is on the house.

威利正在餐廳向一位服務生抱怨。

服務生：是的，先生。有什麼能為你服務的嗎？

威利：我認為我的湯裡有一根頭髮。

服務生：我對此感到非常抱歉，先生。我會馬上為你再送上另一碗湯。湯就由店家免費招待。

🎧 **19-3**

Daphne is making a complaint to a server in a steak house.

Daphne: Excuse me.

Server: Yes, ma'am?

Daphne: My steak is overcooked. It is chewy and tough. And look at this! The vegetables are obviously not fresh.

Server: I'm sorry, ma'am. Let me take them away for you. I'll ask the chef to prepare another one for you.

黛芙妮正在牛排館向一位服務生抱怨。

黛芙妮：不好意思。

服務生：是的，女士？

黛芙妮：我的牛排煮太熟了。既難咬又難切。還有看看這個！這蔬菜顯然不新鮮。

服務生：抱歉，女士。讓我為你撤走它們。我會請主廚再為你準備一份。

🎧 **19-4**

Vincent is making a complaint to a server in a coffee shop.

Server: Here's your chocolate cake, sir. (*Dropping the cake and staining Vincent's jacket*) Oops! I'm terribly sorry!

Vincent: Look what you've done to my jacket!

Server: Please accept my apologies! Let me take your jacket and get it cleaned for you.

Vincent: But the chocolate stain won't wash out easily.

Server: I assure you that I will send it to a professional laundry and cover the cost. I'm really sorry about it.

文森正在咖啡廳向一位服務生抱怨。

服務生：這是你的巧克力蛋糕，先生。(掉了蛋糕並弄髒文森的夾克) 哎呀！非常抱歉！

文森：看看你把我的夾克弄成什麼樣了！

服務生：請接受我的道歉！讓我把你的夾克拿去清理。

文森：但是巧克力漬不容易洗掉。

服務生：我向你保證我會把它送到專業的洗衣店並負擔其費用。我真的很抱歉。

🎧 **19-5**

Ella is making a complaint to a server in a restaurant.

Ella: Could you ask those people at that table to lower their voices? They are really noisy.

Server: I'm sorry, ma'am. I could have you moved to a quieter table. Would that be all right?

Ella: Sure. That would be great.

Server: Please follow me, ma'am. I apologize again for the disturbance.

艾拉正在餐廳向一位服務生抱怨。

艾拉：你可以請那一桌的人說話小聲點嗎？他們真的很吵。

服務生：很抱歉，女士。我能幫你移到比較安靜的桌子。這樣可以嗎？

艾拉：當然。那樣很好。

服務生：請跟我來，女士。我再次為打擾到你感到抱歉。

1. I think there's a hair in my soup.

the soup is not hot enough 這湯不夠熱

my fish is a little dry 我的魚肉有點乾

the cake is too sweet for me 這蛋糕對我而言太甜了

the vegetables are kind of mushy 這蔬菜有點糊爛

this lamb stew tastes off/bad 這燉羊肉味道不對

2. I'll bring you another one right away.

get you a new dish 上一份新的菜給你

take it back to the kitchen right away 馬上把它送回廚房

let the chef know and bring you another one 跟主廚說並再上一份給你

現在才知道

國外用餐不可不知 🔍

當餐廳的餐點難吃或不合你的胃口時，你會向餐廳反應嗎？根據調查，八成顧客不會抱怨，會選擇自認倒楣。說不出口的原因有很多，可能是語言能力有限、不想影響出遊心情或是覺得人生地不熟，少惹麻煩為妙。但是就算是在海外旅遊，還是可以為自己的用餐權益爭取一下喔。只要訴求合理，就不用擔心自己成為奧客。

1. 餐點與菜單內容不符：例如：點魚排卻上成羊排或是餐點被偷工減料，菜單圖片明顯和上桌餐點不符。此時應該要立即和服務生反應，不要自認倒楣默默接受。

2. 餐點與預期不符：特別是在高級餐廳，用餐的品質和服務應該都具有一定的水準。如果覺得餐點太酸、太鹹、太甜、太油膩、有焦味、沒煮熟、煮過頭或甚至出現異物 (像頭髮、蟲子等)，請停止食用並且立刻告知服務生。你可以要求餐廳重上餐點或要求餐廳針對問題餐點不予計費 (但是已經吃完的餐點還是得付費喔)。

3. 服務不好，不付服務費或小費：在多數歐美餐廳用餐，除了要付餐點費用之外，通常也要再給10% 到20% 不等的服務費。但是如果非常不滿意餐廳或服務生的服務，例如：上餐速度極度緩慢或服務生態度不佳等，顧客除了可以馬上向餐廳主管反應外，也有權利決定要不要給服務費或小費。

美食當前篇

要求帳單、
(分開) 結帳

字彙出外景

🎧 20-1

❶ separate *adj.* 各自的，分開的

❷ check *n.* [C] 帳單

❸ itemized bill *n.* [C] 消費帳單明細

❹ cashier *n.* [C] 收銀員

❺ cash desk *n.* [C] 收銀臺

❻ overcharge *vt.* 多收錢

❼ shortchange *vt.* 少找錢

❽ calculate *vt.* 計算

❾ in total *phr.* 總共

❿ come to *phr.* (金額) 合計

⓫ cash *n.* [U] 現金

⓬ bill *n.* [C] 鈔票

⓭ change *n.* [U] 零錢

⓮ payment *n.* [C] 款項

⓯ tip *n.* [C] 小費

⓰ go Dutch *phr.* 各付各的

🎧 20-2

Jimmy is talking with a server in a French restaurant.

Server: How was everything this evening, sir?

Jimmy: Everything was great. Thank you.

Server: Is there anything else I can get for you?

Jimmy: No, thanks. Check, please.

Server: Sure, I'll be right back with your check.

(*After a few minutes*)

Server: Here is your check, sir. You can take it up to the cashier whenever you are ready.

Jimmy: OK. Thank you.

吉米正在法式餐廳與一位服務生談話。

服務生：今晚用餐還愉快嗎，先生？

吉米：非常愉快。謝謝你。

服務生：你還需要些什麼嗎？

吉米：不用了，謝謝。請給我帳單。

服務生：好的，我馬上拿你的帳單來。

(*幾分鐘後*)

服務生：這是你的帳單，先生。你準備好後，隨時可以拿帳單給收銀員。

吉米：好的。謝謝。

🎧 20-3

Katrina is talking with a server in a restaurant.

Katrina: Excuse me. I'd like the check, please.

Server: Of course, ma'am.

Katrina: Could we have separate checks?

Server: No problem. So, that's one chef's special for each and a glass of
　　　　red wine for you. Is that right?

Katrina: Yes, that's right.

Server: OK, ma'am. I'll be right back with your checks.

卡崔娜正在餐廳與一位服務生談話。

卡崔娜：不好意思。請給我帳單。

服務生：沒問題，女士。

卡崔娜：可以給我們各自的帳單嗎？

服務生：沒問題。所以，你們各自點了一份主廚特餐，你還點了一杯紅酒。對嗎？

卡崔娜：是的，沒錯。

服務生：好的，女士。我馬上將你們的帳單拿來。

20-4

Jerry is talking with a cashier in a steak house.

Cashier: Good evening, sir. May I help you?

Jerry: (*Handing over his check*) Yes, how much will this be?

Cashier: Just a moment, please. (*Calculating the bill*) Thank you for
　　　　waiting, sir. It will be $98 in total.

Jerry: $98? I think there's a mistake. I only ordered the New York steak.
　　　Isn't it $55?

Cashier: I'm sorry, sir. I'll check it right away. (*Checking with the
　　　　server*) That should be $60.50, which includes a 10% service
　　　　charge. I'm very sorry for the mistake.

Jerry: Never mind. (*Handing over a $100 bill*)

Cashier: Here is $39.50 in change. Thank you.

傑瑞正在牛排館與一位收銀員談話。

收銀員：晚安，先生。有什麼我能幫你的嗎？

傑瑞：(*遞過他的帳單*) 有的，這樣多少錢？

收銀員：請稍等一下。(*計算帳單*) 讓你久等了，先生。一共是 98 美元。

傑瑞：98 美元？我覺得搞錯了吧。我只點了紐約客牛排。不是 55 美元嗎？

收銀員：抱歉，先生。我馬上核對。(*和服務生核對*) 應該是 60 美元 50 分，包含 10% 的服務費。很抱歉弄錯了。

傑瑞：沒關係。(*遞過一張 100 美元的紙鈔*)

收銀員：找你 39 美元 50 分。謝謝。

還能這樣說

1. Check, please.

I'd like the check, please. 請給我帳單。

Bring me the check, please. 請給我帳單。

May I have the check, please? 可以麻煩給我帳單嗎？

2. Could we have separate checks?

Could we pay separately? 我們可以分開結帳嗎？

Could we pay our own share? 我們可以結各自的部分嗎？

Please split the check. 請拆開來結帳。

 說到分開結帳，可能會馬上想到 AA 制 (arithmetic average)，但英文可不是這樣用。若想要和朋友各付各的可以說：「Let's go Dutch!」或「Let's go halves!」

3. How much will this be?

How much is it? 這樣多少錢？

How much is the check? 帳單是多少錢？

How much is the total? 一共是多少錢？

How much shall I pay? 我要付多少錢呢？

現在才知道

餐廳結帳不 NG 🔍

誤用中式英文，會讓人一頭霧水，聽不懂你在說什麼喔！

以下是結帳時常常誤用的中式英文，請不要再搞錯啦！

1. 多少錢不是「How much?」：雖然直覺容易想到「How much?」，但在國外餐廳結帳時，請不要這樣用。因為外國人重視隱私，服務生遞交帳單時，通常不會直接跟顧客說金額，而顧客也不會直接問價錢。若在小吃攤詢價也請把句子說完整「How much is it?」

2. 要結帳不是「May I pay?」：雖然下意識會以為是「我可以結帳嗎？」的意思，但其實它的意思比較接近「我可以付這筆錢嗎？」所以服務生聽到這句可能心想「吃飯本來就該付錢，為什麼還要問可不可以付錢，難道可以不付錢就走人嗎？」。因此結帳請說「Check, please.」或「May we have the check, please?」

3. 要請客不是「I'll pay.」：可以用「It's on me.」、「My treat.」或「I'm buying/paying today.」

購物專家篇

瀏覽商品、
推薦商品、
詢問位置

🎧 **21-1**

❶ opening hours *n.* (*pl.*) 營業時間

❷ opening time *n.* [U] 開始營業時間

❸ closing time *n.* [U] 結束營業時間

❹ clerk/salesclerk/salesperson
n. [C] 售貨員

❺ browse *vi.* 隨便看看

❻ look around *phr.* 閒逛，四處看看

❼ in particular *phr.* 特別

❽ recommendation *n.* [C] 推薦

❾ suggestion *n.* [C] 建議

❿ feature *vt.* 以…為特色

⓫ merchandise *n.* [U] 商品，貨物

⓬ souvenir *n.* [C] 紀念品

⓭ display *n.* [C][U] (商品) 陳列，展示

⓮ section *n.* [C] 區

⓯ shelf *n.* [C] 架子

⓰ aisle *n.* [C] 通道

⓱ stock *n.* [U] 庫存

⓲ in stock *phr.* 有存貨

⓳ out of stock *phr.* 售完

🎧 21-2

Adney is talking with a clerk in a shop.

Clerk: Are you looking for anything in particular, sir?

Adney: No, I'm just browsing.

Clerk: If you need any help, please let me know.

Adney: OK. Thanks.

愛德尼正在商店裡和店員談話。

店員：先生，你在特別找什麼東西嗎？

愛德尼：沒有，我只是隨便看看。

店員：如果你需要任何幫助，請讓我知道。

愛德尼：好的。謝謝。

🎧 21-3

Alex is talking with a clerk in a gift shop.

Alex: Hi, I'm looking for some souvenirs for my family and friends. Do you have any recommendations?

Clerk: How about the souvenirs featuring the black bear?

Alex: They're so cute. I'll take five of them. Do you have refrigerator magnets?

Clerk: You can find them in the second aisle. Just next to the key chains and postcards.

艾力克斯正在禮品店裡和店員談話。

艾力克斯：嗨，我在找一些要送給我家人和朋友的紀念品。你有任何推薦嗎？

店員：以黑熊為特色的紀念品如何？

艾力克斯：它們很可愛。我要買五個。你們有冰箱磁鐵嗎？

店員：你可以在第二條通道找到它們。就在鑰匙圈和明信片旁邊。

🎧 21-4

Emma is talking with a clerk in a shoe store.

Emma: Hi. I need a pair of casual shoes. What do you recommend?

Clerk: You could buy loafers. They are casual and comfortable.

Emma: That sounds like what I need. Where are they?

Clerk: You can find them in the section over there.

艾瑪正在鞋店裡和店員談話。

艾瑪：你好。我需要一雙休閒鞋。你推薦什麼鞋？

店員：你可以買樂福鞋。它們既休閒又舒適。

艾瑪：那聽起來像是我所需要的。它們在哪邊？

店員：你可以在那邊的區域找到。

🎧 21-5

Viola is talking with a clerk in a supermarket.

Viola: Excuse me, where can I find milk?

Clerk: You can find it down the aisle. It's next to the frozen food section.

Viola: Is butter there as well?

Clerk: Yes, ma'am.

Viola: What about chocolate? I could not find any.

Clerk: That would be in aisle 5. You will see it on the shelf.

薇奧拉正在超市裡和店員談話。

薇奧拉：不好意思，我在哪裡可以找到牛奶？

店員：你可以在這條走道盡頭找到它。它在冷凍食品區旁邊。

薇奧拉：奶油也在那裡嗎？

店員：是的，女士。

薇奧拉：那巧克力呢？我都找不到。

店員：那在五號通道。你會在架上看到它。

還能這樣說

1. I'm just browsing.

> looking around 四處看看
> having a look around 四處看看
> window-shopping 看看商店櫥窗 (無意購買)

2. Excuse me, where can I find milk?

> can you tell me where I can find spices? 你可以告訴我哪裡可以找到辛香料嗎？
> I'm looking for batteries. Do you have any? 我在找電池。你們有賣嗎？
> do you have any watches? 你們有賣手錶嗎？

3. That would be in aisle 5.

> That should be 那應該是在
> You can find it 你可以找到它

> the dairy section 乳製品區
> the seafood section 海鮮區
> the frozen food section 冷凍食品區
> the produce section 農產品區
> the bakery section 麵包區
> the deli section 熟食區
> the canned food section 罐頭食品區

現在才知道

常見的外國商店種類

出國旅遊除了欣賞美景和大啖美食外，購物當然也是很重要的一環囉！不管是服飾、名產或紀念品等，都讓人很心動。但是你知道要去哪裡才能買到你想要的東西嗎？快來一起了解各類型商店吧！

1. 雜貨店 (grocery store)：販賣蔬果、糧油食品和家庭用品等。

2. 蔬菜水果店 (greengrocer's)：專門販賣蔬菜水果。

3. 肉舖 (butcher's)：專門賣肉類，包括生鮮肉類、香腸、火腿等。

4. 麵包店 (bakery)：販賣麵包、蛋糕和點心等。

5. 精品店 (boutique)：販賣流行、時尚服飾的店，主要賣衣服、鞋子和飾品等。

6. 藥房 (drugstore)：販賣保健品、化妝保養品以及生活用品等，類似藥妝店。

7. 藥房 (pharmacy)：可以配藥和賣藥的藥房。通常醫生開立處方箋後，病人會拿著處方箋到藥房拿藥。一般會有常駐的藥劑師 (pharmacist)，店內也會販售保健品及成藥。

8. 百貨公司 (department store)：販賣各式各樣商品的大型零售商店，常見的部門有男／女／童裝部 (men's/women's/children's clothing department)、化妝品部 (cosmetics department)、居家用品部 (household goods department)、家電產品部 (home electronics department)、美食廣場 (food court) 等。

9. 大型超級市場 (hypermarket)：百貨公司結合超級市場，通常位於城郊。貨物種類繁多，一次就可以買齊所有的物品，可滿足多數消費者的購物需求。

10. 暢貨購物中心 (outlet mall)：集中多個品牌的專櫃或專賣店，並結合餐廳或遊樂設施而形成的大型綜合購物中心，大多位於郊區。銷售的商品主要是零碼、過季商品等，因為價格優惠而廣受消費者歡迎。

購物專家篇

Unit
22

購買衣物：
詢問尺寸、
款式、
試穿衣物、
修改衣物

🎧 **22-1**

① fitting/changing room *n.* [C] 試衣間

② clothing *n.* [U] 衣服

③ top *n.* [C] 上衣

④ suit *n.* [C] 西裝，套裝

⑤ shirt *n.* [C] (男) 襯衫

⑥ blouse *n.* [C] (女) 襯衫

⑦ pants/trousers *n.* (*pl.*) 褲子

⑧ jeans *n.* (*pl.*) 牛仔褲

⑨ style *n.* [C][U] 流行款式

⑩ size *n.* [C][U] 尺寸，尺碼

⑪ skintight *adj.* 緊身的

⑫ tight *adj.* 緊的

⑬ loose *adj.* 鬆的

⑭ try sth on *phr.* 試穿…

⑮ fit *vi.*; *vt.* 合身

⑯ alter *vt.* 修改 (衣服)

⑰ inch *n.* [C] 英寸 (= 2.54 公分)

⑱ change into *phr.* 換上 (衣物)

⑲ hem *vt.* 給…縫摺邊

字彙出外景

141

22-2

Spencer is talking with a clerk in a clothing store.

Spencer: This suit looks nice. What color does this come in?

Clerk: It's one of the new fall collections. We also have it in dark blue.

Spencer: Could I try both on?

Clerk: Certainly. The fitting room is next to the counter.

史賓賽正在服飾店裡和店員談話。

史賓賽：這套西裝看起來很好看。還有其他顏色嗎？

店員：這是秋季新裝。它也有深藍色。

史賓賽：我能試穿這兩套嗎？

店員：當然可以。試衣間在櫃臺旁邊。

22-3

Dan is talking with a clerk in a clothing store.

Dan: I'm looking for a white shirt with long sleeves. Do you have any?

Clerk: Yes, we have several styles in white. I can get one for you to try on. What size do you need?

Dan: My size is 40.

(*After a while*)

Clerk: How does it fit?

Dan: It's a bit tight here. Could I try the next size up?

丹正在服飾店裡和店員談話。

丹：我要找長袖的白色襯衫。你們有賣嗎？

店員：有的，我們有幾款白色襯衫。我能拿一件讓你試穿。你要什麼尺寸？

丹：我的尺寸是四十號。

(*過了一會兒*)

店員：合身嗎？

丹：這裡有點緊。我可以試穿大一號的嗎？

Vanessa is talking with a clerk in a clothing store.

Vanessa: Hi. I'm looking for a pair of skintight jeans.

Clerk: We have some nice black and blue jeans here. These colors are always in style.

Vanessa: Well, I actually prefer blue jeans.

Clerk: Would you like to try them on to see if they fit?

Vanessa: OK.

(*After a while*)

Vanessa: They all fit me well, but I look fat in them. I'll think about it.

凡妮莎正在服飾店裡和店員談話。

凡妮莎：嗨。我想找一條緊身的牛仔褲。

店員：我們這裡有幾條很棒的黑色和藍色的牛仔褲。這些顏色一直都很流行。

凡妮莎：嗯，我其實比較喜歡藍色的牛仔褲。

店員：你要試穿看看是否合身嗎？

凡妮莎：好啊。

(*過了一會兒*)

凡妮莎：穿起來很合身，但我看起來胖胖的。我再考慮看看。

🎧 22-5

Thera is talking with a clerk in a clothing store.

Thera: Excuse me. I'd like to have the pants altered.

Clerk: Do they need to be shortened or lengthened?

Thera: I'd like to have them shortened by about 2 inches.

Clerk: Please change into the pants. I need to mark them for hemming.

席拉正在服飾店裡和店員談話。

席拉：不好意思。我想要修改這條褲子。

店員：要改短還是加長？

席拉：我想要改短約兩英寸。

店員：請你換上褲子。為了縫摺邊，我需要標示褲子。

購物專家篇│購買衣物：詢問尺寸、款式、試穿衣物、修改衣物

還能這樣說

1. What color does this come in?

> What size does this come in? 這件還有什麼尺寸？
>
> What other sizes/colors are available? 還有其他哪些尺寸／顏色有貨呢？
>
> Do you have it in any other sizes/colors? 你們這件還有其他尺寸／顏色嗎？

2. I'm looking for a white shirt with long sleeves. Do you have any?

a	blouse (女) 襯衫	a pair of	pants 長褲
	hoodie 帽 T		shorts 短褲
	knitwear 針織衫		sandals 涼鞋
	jacket 夾克		flats 平底鞋
	coat 外套，大衣		sneakers 球鞋
	trench coat 風衣外套		boots 靴子
	skirt 裙子		high heels 高跟鞋
	dress 洋裝		flip-flops 夾腳拖鞋

3. Could I try the next size up?

> try the next size down 試小一號的
>
> get this in a size nine 試九號的
>
> get this in a small/medium/large size 試小／中／大號的

> ❗ 除了小、中、大號之外，你可能還會看到特小號 (extra small)、特特小號 (double extra small)、特大號 (extra large) 以及特特大號 (double extra large)。

現在才知道

鞋碼對照表（僅供參考） 🔍

女鞋			男鞋		
日本 (JP)	歐洲 (EU)	美國 (US)	日本 (JP)	歐洲 (EU)	美國 (US)
22	34	5	22	34	4
22.5	35	5.5	22.5	35	4.5
23	36	6	23	36	5
23.5	37	6.5	23.5	37	5.5
24	38	7	24	38	6
24.5	39	7.5	24.5	39	6.5
25	40	8	25	40	7
25.5	41	8.5	25.5	41	7.5
26	41	9	26	41	8
26.5	42	9.5	26.5	42	8.5
27	43	10	27	43	9
27.5	44	10.5	27.5	44	9.5
28	44	11	28	44	10
28.5	45	11.5	28.5	45	10.5
29	45	12	29	45	11

 雖然有鞋碼對照表可以參考，但各國、各品牌、甚至各鞋款的鞋子尺寸都會有些許差異。因此在購買鞋子時，建議能試穿就試穿看看，以免買到不合腳的鞋子。

購物專家篇─購買衣物、詢問尺寸、款式、試穿衣物、修改衣物

購物專家篇

特價優惠、
討價還價

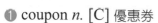

字彙出外景

🎧 **23-1**

① coupon *n.* [C] 優惠券

② list price *n.* [C] 定價

③ sale price *n.* [C] 促銷價

④ fixed price *n.* [C] 不二價

⑤ a special on sth *phr.* …在特價

⑥ special offer *n.* [C] 特價

⑦ promotion *n.* [C][U] 促銷

⑧ anniversary sale *n.* [C] 週年慶特賣

⑨ clearance sale *n.* [C] 清倉特賣

⑩ closing-down sale *n.* [C] 歇業特賣

⑪ cut down *phr.* 減少

⑫ off *adv.* (從…) 扣掉，減去

⑬ offer *vt.* 出價；*n.* [C] (短期的) 折扣

⑭ bargain *vi.* 討價還價；*n.* [C] 特價商品

⑮ pricey *adj.* 昂貴的

⑯ worth *adj.* 值得…

⑰ on sale *phr.* 特價的

⑱ for sale *phr.* 出售的

🎧 23-2

Sophia is talking with a clerk in a drugstore.

Clerk: Hello. How may I help you?

Sophia: Hi, I just received some coupons. I would like to know more information about this lipstick.

Clerk: OK. The list price of this lipstick is $40. With this coupon, you can buy two and get one free.

Sophia: It sounds great! How about this coupon?

Clerk: This coupon is for $3 off sunscreen.

蘇菲亞正在藥妝店裡和店員談話。

店員：你好。有什麼能為你服務的嗎？

蘇菲亞：嗨，我剛才收到一些優惠券。我想知道更多關於這個口紅的訊息。

店員：好的。這支口紅的定價是 40 美元。你用這張優惠券就可以買二送一喔。

蘇菲亞：聽起來不錯！那這張優惠券呢？

店員：用這張優惠券買防曬乳可折抵 3 美元。

🎧 23-3

Renee is talking with a street vendor.

Renee: Hi. How much does this pair of earrings cost?

Vendor: $60.

Renee: I'm interested in the earrings, but they're too pricey. Could you cut the price down a little bit?

Vendor: What are you offering for them?

Renee: Would you sell them for $40?

Vendor: Could you meet me halfway? $50 is my best price. These handmade earrings are worth this price.

芮妮正在和街頭小販談話。

芮妮：嗨。這副耳環要多少錢呢？

小販：60 美元。

芮妮：我對這耳環很感興趣，但太貴了。價錢能便宜一點嗎？

小販：你要出價多少？

芮妮：你能賣 40 美元嗎？

小販：我們可以各退一步嗎？50 美元是我的最低價。這些手工耳環值這個價錢。

🎧 **23-4**

Rupert is talking with a clerk in a shop.

Clerk: Is there anything I can help you with today?

Rupert: Yes. Is there any discount on this jacket?

Clerk: We have a special on jackets today. You will get a 30% discount.

Rupert: It's a real bargain. I'll take it. And how about this sweater?

Clerk: It's on sale, too. You can buy one and get the second one 50% off.

Rupert: That's a good deal. I'll take the gray and the green one.

Clerk: And you'll get a free backpack if you make a purchase over $200.

魯伯特正在商店裡和店員談話。

店員：今天有什麼我可以幫你的嗎？

魯伯特：有的。請問這件夾克有折扣嗎？

店員：夾克今天在特價。你可以享有七折優惠。

魯伯特：真便宜。我要買了。那這件毛衣呢？

店員：這也在特價。你買兩件的話，第二件打五折。

魯伯特：真划算。那我要灰的和綠的各一件。

店員：此外，如果你消費超過 200 美元的話，你會得到一個免費的後背包。

中文和英文表示折扣的方式恰好相反，例如：20% off，是指減少 20% 的費用，就是打八折的意思。所以看到 20% off 時，不要誤以為是打兩折喔！

另外，up to 是表示「⋯折起」，例如：up to 40% off 表示「六折起」，可不要以為全部都六折喔！

還能這樣說

1. You can buy two and get one free.

> You will get a 30% discount. 你可以享有七折優惠。
>
> All items are 10% off. 所有品項打九折。
>
> You can buy one and get the second one 50% off.
> 你買兩件的話,第二件打五折。
>
> For ten more dollars, you can get this product free.
> 再加 10 美元,你就能免費得到這項商品。

2. Could you cut the price down a little bit?

> cut the price a little 降點價
>
> give me a discount 幫我打折
>
> make it a little cheaper 算便宜一點
>
> give me a better price 給我優惠一點的價格

現在才知道
這樣撿便宜最划算 🔍

在美國購物,就要趁折扣季!許多國際和美國品牌會推出期間限定的折扣。價格通常都比臺灣便宜許多。以下是美國的折扣季,大家可以看準時機搶購喔。

1. 情人節 (2/14):商家會看準送禮商機推出優惠。沒有情人也可以趁機撿便宜喔!

2. 復活節 (3～4 月):主要折扣商品為童裝和婦幼用品。由於每年復活節的日期不一定,想要搶購的人可以在出發前再確認時間喔。

3. 陣亡將士紀念日 (5 月的最後一個星期一):三天連假加上換季,商家會推出折扣。

4. 獨立紀念日 (7/4):在美國國慶日這天,商家會推出十分誘人的優惠折扣,堪稱是上半年最大的折扣季。

5. 萬聖節 (10/31):萬聖節免不了變裝派對。零食糖果、派對小物、變裝道具都會有特惠價格喔。

6. 黑五購物節 (11 月的第 4 個星期五):感恩節的隔天是黑色星期五 (Black Friday),而感恩節的下個星期一為「網購星期一」(Cyber Monday)。這段時間可以說是美國全年最大的折扣季,實體店家及網購電商都會祭出殺到見骨的折扣。

黑色星期五 (Black Friday) 的由來:
感恩節假期後,人們要開始為聖誕節採購,因此店家生意都會不錯。而記帳時紅色代表虧損;黑色代表盈餘。所以感恩節的隔天便稱為黑色星期五。這可和西方國家迷信的 13 號星期五 (黑色星期五) 沒有關係喔。

7. 聖誕節 (12/25):聖誕節後到跨年是全年最後折扣季。很多商家都會推出限定商品、聖誕禮盒等折扣商品。

購物專家篇

詢問保固、
商品結帳、
配送服務、
退貨退款

 字彙出外景

🎧 24-1

❶ register *n.* [C] 收銀機

❷ checkout *n.* [C] (尤指大型食品商店的)
結帳處,收銀臺

❸ express lane *n.* [C] 快速結帳通道

❹ warranty *n.* [C] (商品的) 保證書

❺ extended warranty
n. [C] (商品的) 延長保固

❻ money-back guarantee
n. [C] 不滿意退款保證

❼ cover *vt.* 包含

❽ defect *n.* [C] 瑕疵

❾ faulty/defective *adj.* 有瑕疵的

❿ properly *adv.* 正常地,正確地

⓫ return *vt.* 退回 (商品)

⓬ return policy *n.* [C] 退貨政策

⓭ non-returnable *adj.* 無法退還的

⓮ exchange *vt.* 換 (貨)

⓯ exchange period *n.* [C] 換貨期限

⓰ refund *vt.* 退 (款);*n.* [C] 退款

🎧 24-2

Quincy is talking with a clerk in a shop.

Quincy: Excuse me. How long is the warranty on this computer? And what does it cover?

Clerk: We provide a one-year warranty which covers manufacturing defects and free pickup and delivery repair service.

Quincy: How long does it usually take if it needs repairing?

Clerk: People can get the repaired computer back in one to two weeks on average. We have some branches in Taiwan that can carry out maintenance. Here is their information.

Quincy: It sounds good. I'll take this computer.

昆西正在商店裡和店員談話。

昆西：不好意思。請問這臺電腦的保固期有多久？還有保固包含哪些內容呢？

店員：我們提供一年保固，包含製造瑕疵及免費的到府收送的維修服務。

昆西：如果這臺電腦需要維修的話，通常要花多久時間？

店員：大家在平均一至兩週內就能收到修好的電腦。我們在臺灣有一些分店，他們可以進行維修。這裡是他們的資料。

昆西：聽起來不錯。我要買這臺電腦。

🎧 24-3

Regina is talking with a clerk at a checkout.

Regina: Hi, I'd like to buy these pairs of socks.

Clerk: OK, that'll be $19.99, please.

Regina: Could I pay by traveler's check?

Clerk: Sorry. We don't accept checks.

Regina: OK. I'll pay by credit card then. Here's my credit card.

Clerk: Have you checked the size of them? According to our return policy, they're non-returnable.

Regina: Yes, I've checked each of them.

(*After a while*)

Clerk: Thank you. Here is your receipt.

Regina: Thanks.

蕾吉娜正在結帳處和店員談話。

蕾吉娜：你好，我想買這幾雙襪子。

店員：好的，一共是 19 美元 99 分。

蕾吉娜：我可以用旅行支票付款嗎？

店員：抱歉。我們不收支票。

蕾吉娜：好吧。那我用信用卡付款。這是我的信用卡。

店員：你確認過它們的尺寸了嗎？根據我們的退貨政策，它們是不能退還的喔。

蕾吉娜：是的，我每雙都確認過了。

(*過了一會兒*)

店員：謝謝你。這裡是你的收據。

蕾吉娜：謝謝。

 24-4

Payne is talking with a cashier in a shop.

Payne: Excuse me. I'd like to return this handheld game console.

Cashier: OK. Do you have the receipt?

Payne: Here you are.

Cashier: May I ask why you're returning it?

Payne: It doesn't work properly.

Cashier: All right. Would you like to exchange it?

Payne: No. I'd like a refund, please.

Cashier: No problem.

派恩正在商店裡和收銀員談話。

派恩：不好意思。我想退回這臺掌上型遊戲機。

收銀員：好的。你有收據嗎？

派恩：在這裡。

收銀員：請問你為什麼要退貨呢？

派恩：它無法正常運作。

收銀員：好的。你想要換貨嗎？

派恩：不。我想要退款，謝謝。

收銀員：沒問題。

1. Excuse me. How long is the warranty on this computer?

What's the warranty period for this computer? 這臺電腦的保固期多長？

Does this computer come with a warranty? 這臺電腦有保固嗎？

What kind of warranty do you offer? 你們提供哪種保固？

2. It doesn't work properly.

The button is broken. 按鍵壞了。

The remote doesn't work. 遙控器無法運作。

The smartphone is defective. 智慧型手機有瑕疵。

The electric fan turns off by itself. 電風扇自己關掉。

The computer has been freezing up a lot lately. 電腦最近常常當機。

The milk goes sour. 牛奶變酸了。

The blueberries are moldy. 藍莓發霉了。

The bread has gone bad. 麵包已經變質了。

The noodles smell off. 麵條聞起來變質了。

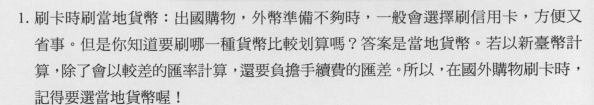

現在才知道

海外消費教戰手則 🔍

1. 刷卡時刷當地貨幣：出國購物，外幣準備不夠時，一般會選擇刷信用卡，方便又省事。但是你知道要刷哪一種貨幣比較划算嗎？答案是當地貨幣。若以新臺幣計算，除了會以較差的匯率計算，還要負擔手續費的匯差。所以，在國外購物刷卡時，記得要選當地貨幣喔！

 海外刷卡通常需要負擔手續費，所以可以鎖定使用有提供海外刷卡回饋的信用卡，貨比三家，說不定有意想不到的優惠喔！

2. 要求運送：在國外購物時，如果你買的商品數量較多或體積較大時，可以詢問店家是否提供運送服務。有的商店有提供海外寄送服務；若只有提供國內寄送服務，可以選擇寄送到飯店或機場，這樣就不用扛著大包小包跑行程囉。

購物專家篇

購買票券、
選擇座位、
預約(語音)
導覽、排隊

 字彙出外景

🎧 **25-1**

① ticket office/booth/counter
n. [C] 售票處

② box office *n.* [C] 售票處

③ ticket agent *n.* [C] 售票員

④ ticket collector *n.* [C] 驗票員

⑤ admission *n.* [U] 入場費；入場資格

⑥ cinema *n.* [C] 電影院

⑦ theater *n.* [C] 劇院

⑧ concert hall *n.* [C] 音樂廳

⑨ sell out *phr.* 賣光

⑩ guided tour *n.* [C] 導覽

⑪ individual tour *n.* [C] 個人導覽

⑫ group tour *n.* [C] 團體導覽

⑬ audio tour/guide *n.* [C] 語音導覽

⑭ information counter
n. [C] (諮詢) 服務臺

⑮ line *n.* [C] 排隊隊伍

⑯ stand/wait in line for sth *phr.* 為⋯排隊

⑰ cut in line *phr.* 插隊

🎧 **25-2**

Parker is talking with a ticket agent at the ticket office.

Parker: Hi, I'd like to buy one adult pass and two student passes. What do the passes include?

Agent: Both kinds of passes include all-day admission to the amusement park and unlimited entrance to all rides and shows.

Parker: When do you close today?

Agent: We close at 10:00 p.m.

Parker: How much do the passes cost?

Agent: An adult pass is $60 and a student pass is $45. So, the total comes to $150.

Parker: Alright, here is $150.

派克正在售票處和售票員談話。

派克：嗨，我想買一張成人票和兩張學生票。這些票包含了什麼？

售票員：兩種票都包含全天入園資格和不限次數搭乘遊樂設施及觀看表演。

派克：你們今天幾點閉園？

售票員：我們晚上十點閉園。

派克：票價是多少？

售票員：成人票是 60 美元，學生票是 45 美元。所以，總共 150 美元。

派克：好的，這裡是 150 美元。

🎧 **25-3**

Queena is talking with a ticket agent at the ticket office.

Queena: Hi, I'd like two tickets for the magic show.

Agent: For what time?

Queena: 1:30 p.m., please.

Agent: Sorry. All the tickets are sold out. Do you want another time?

Queena: Do you have any tickets available for the 5:00 p.m. show?

Agent: Yes. Two tickets, right?

Queena: That's right. Could I have center seats?

Agent: Sure. In the middle or on the aisle?

Queena: An aisle seat, please.

昆娜正在售票處和售票員談話。

昆娜：嗨，我要買兩張魔術表演的票。

售票員：要什麼時間的呢？

昆娜：請給我下午一點半的票。

售票員：抱歉。票都賣光了。你想要其他時間的嗎？

昆娜：你們下午五點的表演還有座位嗎？

售票員：有的。你要兩張票，對吧？

昆娜：沒錯。可以給我中區的座位嗎？

售票員：沒問題。中間還是靠走道的呢？

昆娜：請給我靠走道的座位。

 25-4

Oscar is talking with a clerk in the museum.

Oscar: Excuse me. Do you have any guided tours or audio guides?

Clerk: Yes. Our next group tour will begin in twenty minutes, and we also provide audio guide equipment.

Oscar: Is the audio guide available in Chinese?

Clerk: Yes. You can rent the device at the information counter.

奧斯卡正在博物館裡和職員談話。

奧斯卡：不好意思。你們有導覽或是語音導覽嗎？

職員：有的。我們下一場團體導覽將在二十分鐘之後開始，我們也提供語音導覽器材。

奧斯卡：語音導覽有中文的嗎？

職員：有的。你可以在服務臺租借設備。

There is a long line at the ticket office, and Jean and Hank are waiting in line for tickets.

Jean: Oh, my goodness! Look at the crowd! We have to stand in line for at least half an hour to get the tickets.

Hank: You bet! It's boiling hot. I will go and buy some cold drinks.

Jean: Get me a Coke, thanks.

Hank: OK. I'll be right back. Make sure nobody cuts in line.

Jean: No problem.

售票處大排長龍，而珍和漢克正在排隊買票。

珍：喔，我的天呀！看看這人群！我們要排至少半小時才買得到票。

漢克：沒錯！天氣好熱。我去買一些冷飲。

珍：幫我買一瓶可樂，謝謝。

漢克：好的。我馬上回來。確保沒人插隊。

珍：沒問題。

 排隊時若要禮讓別人優先，請說「After you.」而不是「You go first.」喔！因為「You go first.」帶有命令的口吻，反而是不恰當的用法喔！

 還能這樣說

1. I'd like to buy one adult pass and two student passes.

a child pass 兒童票	a disabled ticket 愛心票
a night pass 星光票	twenty group tickets 二十張團體票
a senior ticket 敬老票	a one-day ticket 一日票

2. I'd like two tickets for the magic show.

tonight's performance 今晚的表演
next Saturday's concert 下週六的音樂會

現在才知道

市區觀光好方便 🔍

想要自助旅行，自由安排行程，卻又不知道從何下手嗎？那市區觀光 (city tour) 絕對是你的最佳選擇！旅客可以依照個人喜好，挑選幾個喜歡的當地市區觀光行程，由當地導遊講解地方文化和歷史，帶你探索該地區的人文風情。

以下是選擇市區觀光時，可以考量的幾個項目。

1. 市區觀光的主題，例如：美食探索、歷史文化等。

2. 行程內容及包含哪些景點。

3. 行程總共需要多少時間。

4. 集合的時間與地點。

5. 行程的總價格，且須留意費用是否包含餐費、交通等。

四通八達篇

詢問路線、
查閱地圖、
搭錯車

 字彙出外景

🎧 26-1

❶ ask (sb) for directions *phr.* (向…) 問路

❷ give (sb) directions *phr.* (給…) 指路

❸ turn right/left *phr.* 右／左轉

❹ block *n.* [C] 街區

❺ junction/intersection *n.* [C] 交叉路口

❻ crossroads/intersection *n.* [C] 十字路口

❼ signpost *n.* [C] 路標

❽ landmark *n.* [C] 地標

❾ stoplight/traffic light
   n. [C] 紅綠燈，交通號誌燈

❿ zebra crossing *n.* [C] 斑馬線

⓫ crosswalk/pedestrian crossing
   n. [C] 行人穿越道

⓬ underpass *n.* [C] 地下道

⓭ footbridge *n.* [C] 天橋

⓮ overpass *n.* [C] 高架橋

⓯ highway *n.* [C] 公路

⓰ freeway *n.* [C] 高速公路

⓱ get in/out of 上／下
   phr. (只能乘坐的交通工具，如：汽車)

⓲ get on/off 上／下
   phr. (可站立的交通工具，如：公車、火車)

旅遊狀況句

🎧 26-2

Norton is reading a map on the street.

Passerby: Hi, do you need a hand?

Norton: Yes, please. I am new here. Do you know how to get to the nearest subway station?

Passerby: Sure. It's on Maple Street. Walk two blocks down the street, turn left onto Maple Street, and there's a subway station on your right at the next junction. You won't miss it.

Norton: Is it far from here? Can I go there on foot?

Passerby: It's within walking distance. I think it's a fifteen-minute walk from here.

諾頓正在路上看地圖。

路人：嗨，你需要幫助嗎？

諾頓：好啊，麻煩你。我剛到這裡。你知道要怎麼去最近的地鐵站嗎？

路人：當然。它在楓樹街上。沿著這條路走兩個街區，左轉到楓樹街上，地鐵站在你右邊的下一個交叉路口。你不會錯過它的。

諾頓：離這邊很遠嗎？走路能到嗎？

路人：走路能到。我想從這邊走過去要十五分鐘。

🎧 26-3

Ann is showing a map to a receptionist and asking him for directions.

Ann: How far is the zoo from the hotel?

Receptionist: It isn't far from here. It takes about thirty minutes to get there by car.

Ann: Could you show me the way on this map? (*Showing the map*)

Receptionist: (*Pointing at the map*) Just drive west along Bowen Road. Then go under this freeway overpass. When you get to Garden Road, turn left and keep going. The road will end at the entrance to the zoo.

Ann: Thank you for your help.

Receptionist: I'm glad to help.

安正拿一張地圖向飯店櫃臺接待員問路。

安：動物園離飯店有多遠？

接待員：離這裡不遠。開車大概三十分鐘路程。

安：你能在這張地圖上幫我指路嗎？(*出示地圖*)

接待員：(*指著地圖*) 只要沿著寶文路向西開。然後，從這條高速公路高架橋下開過。你到花園路時左轉且繼續走。這條路的盡頭就是動物園入口。

安：謝謝你的幫忙。

接待員：很高興能幫到你。

 26-4

Stanley is talking with another passenger on a coach.

Stanley: Excuse me. Is this the coach for Portsmouth?

Passenger: No. This is for Bournemouth.

Stanley: Oh, no. I'm on the wrong coach. Where should I get off to change for the right one?

Passenger: You should change at Southampton.

Stanley: OK, thanks. You've saved my day!

史坦利正在客運上和另一名乘客談話。

史坦利：不好意思。這是前往樸茨茅斯的客運嗎？

乘客：不是。這是前往伯恩茅斯的客運。

史坦利：喔，不。我搭錯車了。我應該在哪裡下車換成正確的客運呢？

乘客：你應該在南安普敦換車。

史坦利：好的，謝謝。你幫了我大忙！

還能這樣說

1. Do you know how to get to the nearest subway station?

> the closest post office 最近的郵局
> a nearby police station 附近的警察局
> this famous landmark 這個知名的地標
> the clinic in this neighborhood 這區的診所

2. It's on Maple Street.

> next to a parking lot 在一座停車場旁邊
> near a gas station 靠近一間加油站
> across from a bank 在一間銀行的對面
> on the corner of the street 在街角
> opposite a pharmacy 正對著一間藥局
> on the right/left side of a bookstore 在一間書店的右邊／左邊
> between a florist's and a convenience store 在花店和便利商店之間

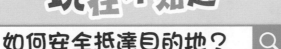

現在才知道

如何安全抵達目的地？ 🔍

四通八達篇 ｜ 詢問路線、查閱地圖、搭錯車

在國外旅遊一定要留意自身安全，否則很容易成為不法分子下手的目標。此外，在國外自駕，除了語言不通導致不易辨識路牌外，不熟悉路況也很容易導致意外。

以下幾招報你知，讓你平平安安地出遊：

1. 善用 Google 地圖等導航網站，事先規劃路線並記錄沿途會經過的路標。如此一來，在前往旅遊地點時，也不會手忙腳亂，找不到方向。

2. 問路要問對人，熟記基本的問路用語並詢問住宿的飯店人員會是比較好的選擇；若是在路途中迷路，也盡量去附近明亮的商店內問路。

3. 即便不知道路，也不要太慌張。如果手上拿著地圖或手機，一臉慌張地找路，就很容易成為歹徒下手的目標。當有太過熱情的路人要為你指路時，也請記得保持適當距離，以免身上的貴重物品被不安好心的人扒走喔。

4. 在市區駕車不要過度依賴導航系統，因為導航系統無法及時更新當地路況，若是遇到道路施工，就可能會把你帶進死胡同或甚至開到對向車道。因此要記得幾條重要道路的相對位置，萬一碰到狀況，也能即時反應，找到替代的方案。

5. 在高速公路迷路時，千萬不要驚慌，可先從最近的交流道離開。回到一般道路或休息站後，可以重新規劃路線或詢問交通警察、休息站人員等。

四通八達篇

詢問位置

字彙出外景

🎧 **27-1**

❶ floor *n.* [C] 樓層

❷ floor plan *n.* [C] (建築物) 平面圖

❸ main door *n.* [C] 大門

❹ hall *n.* [C] 走廊

❺ lounge *n.* [C] 休息廳，等候室

❻ stairs *n.* (*pl.*) 樓梯

❼ lift/elevator *n.* [C] 電梯

❽ (up/down) escalator

   n. [C] (上／下行) 電扶梯

❾ go upstairs/downstairs *phr.* 上／下樓

❿ ladies'/women's room *n.* [C] 女廁

⓫ men's room *n.* [C] 男廁

⓬ (accessible) toilet/restroom

   n. [C] (無障礙) 廁所

⓭ baby care room *n.* [C] 育嬰室

⓮ gift shop *n.* [C] 禮品店

⓯ locker *n.* [C] 置物櫃

⓰ cloakroom *n.* [C] 衣帽寄存處

旅遊狀況句

🎧 27-2

Osmond is talking with a server in an all-you-can-eat restaurant.

Osmond: Excuse me, do you have soft drinks?

Server: Yes, the soda fountain is on the left side of the coffee machine.

Osmond: Thanks. I'm also trying to get some salad.

Server: We have a very nice salad bar—follow me!

奧斯蒙正在一間吃到飽餐廳和服務生談話。

奧斯蒙：不好意思，你們有提供汽水嗎？

服務生：有喔，汽水機在咖啡機的左邊。

奧斯蒙：謝謝。我也想要拿一些沙拉。

服務生：我們有很棒的沙拉吧——跟我來！

🎧 27-3

Phoebe is talking with a clerk in a shopping mall.

Phoebe: Excuse me. I'm looking for the ladies' room. Could you tell me where it is?

Clerk: Of course. It's on the third floor, just next to the stairs.

Phoebe: Is there an escalator that I could take to the third floor?

Clerk: Yes, it's right there. (*Pointing to the escalator*)

菲比正在購物中心和店員談話。

菲比：不好意思。我在找女廁。可以請你告訴我它在哪裡嗎？

店員：當然可以。女廁在三樓，就在樓梯旁邊。

菲比：有電扶梯可以讓我搭到三樓嗎？

店員：有的，就在那裡。(*指向電扶梯*)

Norman is talking with a receptionist in the hotel lounge.

Norman: Pardon me, do you have a business center in the hotel?

Receptionist: Yes, sir. It's on the fifth floor. You can take an elevator to the business center.

Norman: Can you tell me where the elevator is?

Receptionist: Sure. It's in back of the gift shop. Once you get to the fifth floor, turn left. Go down the hall, and you'll see the business center on your right. There's a plate on the door.

Norman: OK, thanks a lot.

Receptionist: You're welcome.

諾曼正在飯店休息廳和接待員談話。

諾曼：不好意思，飯店裡有商務中心嗎？

接待員：有的，先生。在五樓。你可以搭電梯去到商務中心。

諾曼：你可以告訴我電梯在哪裡嗎？

接待員：當然。電梯在禮品店的後面。你一到五樓就左轉。沿著走廊走，你會看到商務中心在你的右邊。門上有一個標示牌。

諾曼：好的，非常感謝你。

接待員：不客氣。

🎧 27-5

Odelia is talking with a clerk in a museum.

Odelia: Sorry to bother you. Do you know how to get to the permanent exhibition hall?

Clerk: Just go down the stairs to the second floor. Then, take a right turn, and you'll see it. Here is the guide map. Maybe you'll need one.

Odelia: OK, thanks for your help.

Clerk: I'm glad to help.

> 奧黛莉亞正在博物館和職員談話。
>
> 奧黛莉亞：抱歉打擾一下，你知道怎麼去常設展廳嗎？
>
> 職員：就走這個樓梯下到二樓。然後右轉，你就會看到了。這導覽地圖給你。
> 　　　或許你會需要一份。
>
> 奧黛莉亞：好的，謝謝你的幫忙。
>
> 職員：很高興幫得上忙。

還能這樣說

1. Could you tell me where it is?

the restaurant 餐廳	the automated teller machine (ATM)
the café/coffee shop 咖啡廳	自動櫃員機，提款機
the dining area 餐飲區	the (accessible) toilet/restroom
the smoking section 吸菸區	(無障礙) 廁所
the non-smoking section 禁菸區	the baby care room 育嬰室
the fire escape 火災逃生梯	the gift shop 禮品店
the emergency exit 緊急出口	the locker 置物櫃
the extinguisher 滅火器	the cloakroom 衣帽寄存處

2. The elevator is in back of the gift shop.

behind 在…後面	beside/next to 在…旁邊
in front of 在…前面	near 在…附近

3. Sorry to bother you, do you know how to get to the permanent exhibition hall?

could you tell me where the gift shop is 你能告訴我禮品店在哪裡嗎

could you tell me the way to the dining area 你能告訴我去餐飲區的路嗎

do you know where the locker is 你知道置物櫃在哪裡嗎

現在才知道

各國樓層大不同 🔍

你知道其實你以為的一樓可能不是一樓嗎！？而國外居然有消失的十三樓！？在國外旅遊時，如果沒有留意，可是很容易被當地的樓層名稱搞得暈頭轉向。

快來看看關於樓層的小知識吧！

1. 他們的一樓其實是我們的二樓：在歐洲 (例如：英國) 或曾被歐洲殖民過的地區，建築物的第一層稱為地面樓層 (ground floor)，在電梯按鈕中顯示為 G；而我們說的二樓才是他們的一樓。

 美國的一樓則和臺灣一樣，指的都是建築物的第一層喔！

2. 在歐美消失的十三樓：在基督教信仰中，數字 13 被認為是不吉利、會招來厄運的數字。因此，多數歐美國家的建築物，例如：飯店、醫院等，會採用 12A 或 14A 等來代替十三樓。

> 華人其實也有類似的忌諱。數字 4 和「死」發音相似，所以去醫院搭電梯時，常會發現沒有四樓的按鈕，樓層號碼會直接跳到五樓。而購屋時也能發現四樓或門牌號碼有四的房屋，價格會稍微低一些。

3. floor、story 和 storey 的區別：雖然這三個字都翻譯為「樓層」，但是 floor 通常是指居住或活動的樓層，使用時前面要搭配序數，例如：3rd floor 三樓。而 story 則指建築物有幾層樓高，前面搭配數字即可，例如：a five-story building 五層樓高的建築物。至於 storey 是英式英語，用法相當於 story。

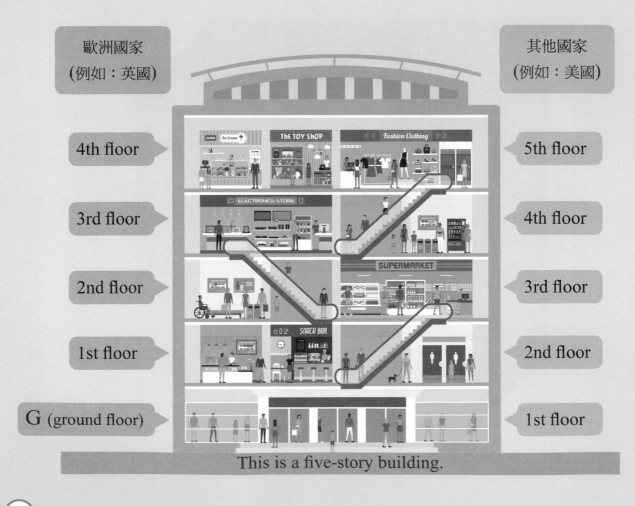

This is a five-story building.

四通八達篇

自駕旅遊：
預約租車、
取車、加油

 字彙出外景　　　🎧 28-1

❶ car rental agency/company

　　n. [C] 租車公司

❷ rent *vi.; vt.* 租 (車)

❸ pick up *phr.* 取 (車)

❹ return/drop off *phr.* 還 (車)

❺ compact *n.* [C] 轎車

❻ sport utility vehicle (SUV)

　　n. [C] 休旅車

❼ van *n.* [C] 廂型車

❽ manual (car) *n.* [C] 手排車

❾ automatic (car) *n.* [C] 自排車

❿ registration (number)/

　　license (plate) number

　　n. [C] 車牌號碼

⓫ (international) driver's license

　　n. [C] (國際) 駕照

⓬ run out (of sth) *phr.* 耗盡，用完 (…)

⓭ gas/petrol station *n.* [C] 加油站

⓮ fill up *phr.* 加滿 (油)

⓯ gas/gasoline/petrol *n.* [U] 汽油

⓰ diesel *n.* [U] 柴油

🎧 28-2

Melissa is talking with a clerk in a car rental agency.

Melissa: Hello, I'd like to rent a car. From May 5th to May 8th.

Clerk: OK. Where would you like to pick it up and drop it off?

Melissa: I need it here, but I'd like to return it in New York City.

Clerk: Sure. You can return it at any of our branches within the country. What type of car would you like?

Melissa: I'll take a compact. How much would it cost per day? Also, do I need to fill the tank up before returning the car?

Clerk: It would cost you $50 per day, including tax and insurance. And yes, please fill it up.

Melissa: OK. I'll take it.

梅麗莎正在租車公司和職員談話。

梅麗莎：你好，我想要租車。五月五日至五月八日。

職員：好的。你想在哪裡取車和還車？

梅麗莎：我要在這裡取車，但我想在紐約市還車。

職員：當然。你可以在國內我們的任一家分店還車。你想要租什麼車款？

梅麗莎：我要轎車。租金一天多少？另外，還車前我需要把油箱加滿嗎？

職員：一天 50 美元，含稅和保險。是的，請加滿油。

梅麗莎：好的。我租了。

🎧 28-3

Morton is talking with a clerk in a car rental company.

Morton: Hi, I'd like to pick up my rental car. My last name is Walker.

Clerk: Oh, yes, Mr. Walker. Did you book a Mitsubishi Mirage for a week?

Morton: Yes. That's correct.

Clerk: May I have your international driver's license and passport?

Morton: OK, there you go.

Clerk: Thank you. (*After a while*) The total, including tax, insurance, and roadside assistance, comes out at $1,200.

Morton: OK. Here is my credit card.

Clerk: Here is the key. Please follow me. We need to check the car.

摩頓正在租車公司和職員談話。

摩頓：嗨，我要取我租的車。我的姓氏是沃克。

職員：喔，是的，沃克先生。你預定了一輛三菱 Mirage，租一星期是吧？

摩頓：是的。沒錯。

職員：可以給我你的國際駕照和護照嗎？

摩頓：好，給你。

職員：謝謝。(過了　會兒) 總費用是 1,200 美元，含稅、保險和道路救援。

摩頓：好的。這是我的信用卡。

職員：這是鑰匙。請跟我來。我們需要查看一下車子。

 28-4

Lesley almost runs out of gas, and she is now at a gas station.

Clerk: What kind of gas would you like?

Lesley: Fill it up with regular unleaded, please.

Clerk: OK. Do you want me to check the tire pressure?

Lesley: No, thank you. I'm in a hurry. How much is it?

Clerk: $40, please.

萊絲莉幾乎用完汽油，而她現在在加油站。

職員：請問你要加哪一種油呢？

萊絲莉：加滿普通無鉛汽油，謝謝。

職員：好的。要我幫你檢查一下胎壓嗎？

萊絲莉：不用了，謝謝你。我趕時間。多少錢？

職員：40 美元，麻煩你。

還能這樣說

1. What type of car would you like?

What type of car are you looking for? 你在找哪一種車款？
Which size of car are you thinking? 你想租哪個尺寸的車？

2. I'll take a compact.

I need an SUV. 我需要一輛休旅車。
A van will be fine for me. 廂型車對我來說很適合。
I want to rent an automatic. 我想要租一輛自排車。
I would like to rent a manual car. 我想要租一輛手排車。

3. How much would it cost per day?

How much is the rental for a week? 一週的租金是多少？
What are your rental rates? 你們的租金是多少？

4. Fill it up with regular unleaded, please.

Put in $20 worth of 加 20 美元的
I need five liters of 我需要五公升的

regular 普通的 midgrade 中級的 premium 高級的	leaded 含鉛的 unleaded 無鉛的	gas/gasoline/petrol 汽油
diesel 柴油		

現在才知道

這樣租車最 FUN 心 🔍

1. 提前申請國際駕照：若出國遊玩選擇自駕，一定要先去各行政區的監理所辦理國際駕照喔！辦理國際駕照時需要準備的證件、照片等相關規定，可至中華民國交通部公路總局或各縣市監理所網站查詢。

 有時在其它國家租車時，也會被要求出示臺灣駕照正本，所以出國時也要帶著喔！但在日本自駕則只需要臺灣駕照及其日文譯本；日文譯本須至國內各公路監理單位申請，不可用自行翻譯的版本喔。

2. 選擇國際或當地知名的連鎖租車公司：如果你是新手，租車時最好先找這類大型的租車公司。除了比較容易事先在網路上找到相關資料，大型租車公司的租還車地點也會有較多的選擇。總之，比較安全、可靠、品質有保障。

3. 了解租借的車種：盡量選擇和平常駕駛相近的車款，這樣比較容易上手。租借時也要問清楚加哪種油和設備的使用方式。必要時也可以請店員現場示範，以免加錯油導致車輛受損或上路卻不會用的窘境。

4. 取車時要詳細檢查車況：通常店員會和你一起查看車況，確認車子外觀是否在租借前就已經有磨損、掉漆等狀況。建議取車時可以拍照或錄影存證，避免還車時產生糾紛。

 也要注意保險桿、底盤等是否有損壞，免得還車時啞巴吃黃連喔。

5. 看清合約和規定：簽約前，一定要清楚了解合約相關規定，例如：還車時是否要加滿油、還車時間、超時費用等。

 雖然玩到最後一秒還車才划算，但建議大家可以提早還車，以免因為人生地不熟，晚還車而被罰款，破壞出遊的好心情。

6. 保險千萬不要省：不管駕駛技術多好，最好都要保旅遊平安險、意外險、車輛失竊、毀損險、第三方責任險和道路緊急服務等。在租車時也可詢問租車公司，租金包含哪些保險，需要自費的保險又有哪些。有時租車公司會推薦一些加保的項目，請仔細比較保險內容，避免重複保險造成不必要的支出喔。

＊警察臨檢時要配合：如果遇到警車尾隨、閃警燈或鳴警笛，請盡快停在路邊安全的地方。停車後，請保持原有坐姿並將雙手放在方向盤上；此時不要解開安全帶，應靜候警察到車邊詢問。請不要主動下車，以免被誤會要襲警。請遵照警察指示並配合問話。若要伸手拿東西，一定要先跟警察說，以免被懷疑要拿武器。不管是否有違反交通規則，千萬不要跟警察爭論，有問題可事後再進行申訴。

 各國國情、法規有所不同，出國前一定要再確認這些細節喔！

四通八達篇

搭乘大眾
運輸工具

 字彙出外景

🎧 **29-1**

❶ subway/metro/the Underground
   n. [C] 地鐵

❷ local/regional train *n.* [C] 區間車

❸ express (train) *n.* [C] 特快列車

❹ platform *n.* [C] 月臺

❺ bus terminal *n.* [C] 巴士總站

❻ schedule/timetable *n.* [C] 時刻表

❼ station staff *n.* [C] [U] 站務人員

❽ route map *n.* [C] 路線圖

❾ refill/top up *vt.* 加值

❿ pass *n.* [C] 乘車證

⓫ ticket (vending) machine
   n. [C] 自動售票機

⓬ ticket gate *n.* [C] 驗票閘門

⓭ line *n.* [C] (地鐵) 路線

⓮ change at sth *phr.* 在⋯換車

⓯ terminate *vi.* 到達終點站

⓰ via *prep.* 經過

Julie is talking with a ticket agent at Rotterdam Central Station.

Julie: I'd like a one-way ticket to Paris, please. And I have to get there by 3:00 p.m. today.

Agent: OK. (*Checking the schedule*) You'll need to take the 11:58 a.m. train, and it will arrive in Paris at 2:35 p.m.

Julie: Sounds great. Does the train stop at every station?

Agent: No, it's express, and you don't have to change. Would you like a first-class or second-class ticket?

Julie: I'll have a second-class ticket, please.

Agent: That will be €150.

Julie: OK. Here's my credit card. Can you tell me which platform I should go to?

Agent: Platform 3.

Julie: Thanks.

茱莉正在鹿特丹中央車站和售票員談話。

茱莉：請給我一張去巴黎的單程票。然後我需要在今天下午三點前到達那裡。

售票員：好的。(查看時刻表) 那你需要搭乘上午十一點五十八分的火車，它會在下午兩點三十五分抵達巴黎。

茱莉：聽起來不錯。火車會每個站都停嗎？

售票員：不，它是特快列車，你不用換車。你要頭等艙還是二等艙的車票呢？

茱莉：請給我二等艙的車票。

售票員：一共是 150 歐元。

茱莉：好的。這是我的信用卡。可以請你告訴我應該要去哪個月臺嗎？

售票員：第三月臺。

茱莉：謝謝。

🎧 29-3

Lewis is talking with a bus driver at the bus terminal.

Lewis: Do you stop anywhere near the Museum of Modern Art?

Driver: Come on in. You can get off at 6th Ave & W 53rd St.

Lewis: (*Getting on the bus*) Thanks a lot. Would you please let me know when we get there?

Driver: Sure.

路易士正在巴士總站和公車司機談話。

路易士：公車會停在現代藝術館附近嗎？

司機：上車吧。你可以在第六大道和西 53 街那站下車。

路易士：(*上公車*) 非常謝謝你。到站時可以麻煩讓我知道嗎？

司機：當然可以。

🎧 29-4

After topping up his card at a ticket machine, Lester is talking with one of the station staff near the ticket gate.

Lester: Excuse me. Could you tell me which line I should take to get to the ferry pier?

Staff: Sure. (*Pointing at the route map*) Take the red line first and change at City Hall Station for the green line. Get on the one terminating at City Zoo Station. That passes via Ferry Pier Station.

Lester: May I know how long it will take me to get there?

Staff: About an hour.

Lester: Thanks a million.

Staff: No problem. Have a nice day.

在售票機加值他的卡之後，萊斯特在驗票閘門附近和站務人員談話。

萊斯特：不好意思。你可以告訴我要搭哪一條線去渡輪碼頭嗎？

站務人員：當然可以。(指著路線圖) 先搭紅線到市政廳站轉綠線。搭上終點站是市立動物園的車。那會經過渡輪碼頭站。

萊斯特：請問去那裡要多久時間？

站務人員：大約一個小時。

萊斯特：太感謝了。

站務人員：不客氣。祝你有美好的一天。

 還能這樣說

1. Do you stop anywhere near the Museum of Modern Art?

Excuse me. Do you stop at City Hall? 不好意思。請問有在市政廳停靠嗎？

Where can I take the bus to Central park? 我能去哪邊搭公車到中央公園？

I want to go to Louvre Meseum. Which bus should I take?
我想去羅浮宮。我應該搭哪輛公車？

2. Excuse me. Could you tell me which line I should take to get to the ferry pier?

How many stops are there to get to Tokyo Station?
到東京車站要經過幾站呢？

Which stop should I get off? 我應該在哪一站下車？

What is the price of a one-day pass? 一日通行證的價格是多少？

Which port does the ferry stop at? 渡船停靠哪個港口？

現在才知道

搭車搭船大補帖 🔍

如果你還沒考取駕照，不能自駕趴趴走，但又崇尚自由，不愛跟團。那麼大眾運輸工具絕對是你出國的最佳旅伴。

以下是一些在國外搭乘大眾運輸工具的注意事項：

1. 公車：搭公車旅遊方便又省錢，但各國公車文化還是有些許差異，因此建議出國前先上網了解喔。例如：紐約的公車站不像臺灣有詳細的路線圖，因此要事先查好公車路線和發車時間。在倫敦，若雙層巴士上層已經客滿，司機可能會廣播請乘客回到下層，如果有人站在上層不走，司機就不會開車。而在日本不用特別揮手，只要看著公車司機或司機看到站牌有人就會靠站；下車時，務必要等車子停妥後再移動，車子尚未停妥就起身走動在日本可是一大忌！

2. 地鐵、捷運：臺灣稱大眾捷運系統為 MRT (Mass Rapid Transit)，簡稱「捷運」。美國和日本為 subway，英國用 the Underground 或 tube，法國則是用 metro。除了代幣或票卡型車票，各國也有類似臺灣的悠遊卡和一卡通的儲值型交通卡，感應進站 (touch in) 或出站 (touch out) 都很快速方便。此外，上下車時，可能會聽到「Mind the gap between the train and the platform. 請小心列車和月臺間的間隙。」是因為月臺間隙真的很大，一個不小心可能就會掉下去或卡住腳！

3. 渡輪：在國外搭乘觀光交通渡輪，也是個有趣的體驗。票種通常會分臥艙 (cabin) 和座位 (seat)，臥艙也有分一等艙 (first-class cabin) 和二等艙 (second-class cabin)。

 如果容易暈車暈船 (motion sickness) 的話，除了看遠方、挑選較前排的座位、避免在交通工具上閱讀等避暈方法外，也可以在搭車或搭船前三十分鐘至一小時服用暈車暈船藥 (motion sickness pills)。但慢性病病患、兒童及孕婦，應經醫師評估，切勿自行購買藥物服用喔！

突發狀況篇

物品協尋、
物品失竊

🎧 30-1

① lost-and-found/lost property office

　　n. [U] 失物招領處

② keep an eye out for sth

　　phr. 注意，留心⋯

③ make contact with sb *phr.* 和⋯聯絡

④ contact *vt.* 聯絡

⑤ turn up *phr.* (遺失後) 突然出現，突然找到

⑥ thief *n.* [C] 小偷

⑦ pickpocket *n.* [C] 扒手

⑧ theft *n.* [C][U] 偷竊

⑨ steal *vt.* 偷

⑩ robber *n.* [C] 搶匪

⑪ robbery *n.* [C][U] 搶劫

⑫ rob *vt.* 搶劫

⑬ emergency

　　n. [C][U] 緊急事件，突發狀況

⑭ describe *vt.* 描述

⑮ valuables *n.* (*pl.*) 貴重物品

⑯ security camera *n.* [C] 監視器

⑰ foot *n.* [C] 呎 (= 30.48 公分)

🎧 **30-2**

Kevin is talking with a clerk at the lost-and-found of a shopping mall.

Kevin: Excuse me, could you help me?

Clerk: Sure. What seems to be the problem?

Kevin: Has anyone turned in a black leather wallet? I have lost mine.

Clerk: I'm afraid not. When was the last time you saw it?

Kevin: About an hour ago. I was in the electrical shop on the seventh floor.

Clerk: Let me call the shop to see if they've found one. (*A Few minutes later*) I'm sorry no one has turned in any wallet there, either. Please fill in this "Lost & Found Property Inquiry Form," and we'll keep an eye out for it. We will make contact with you when it turns up. If you have any debit or credit cards, I suggest you report the loss first.

Kevin: You've been a big help.

凱文正在購物中心的失物招領處跟職員談話。

凱文：不好意思，可以幫幫我嗎？

職員：當然可以。有什麼問題嗎？

凱文：有人拿來一個黑色皮夾嗎？我遺失我的了。

職員：恐怕沒有。你最後一次看到它是什麼時候？

凱文：大約一小時前。我當時在七樓的電器行。

職員：我打電話給那家店，看看他們有沒有發現皮夾。(幾分鐘後) 抱歉，那邊也沒有人找到你的皮夾。請填寫這份「找尋遺失物處理單」，我們會持續幫你留意。找到它時，我們會聯絡你。如果你有任何金融卡或信用卡，我建議你先掛失。

凱文：你幫我大忙了。

🎧 30-3

Isabel is reporting the theft to the police.

Officer: Could you tell me when your bag was stolen?

Isabel: I think a thief took it away when I had lunch at the Joyce Café at noon.

Officer: Have you lost any valuables?

Isabel: I had $500 in cash, a camera, and my passport in the bag.

Officer: OK, we will check the security cameras. We'll contact you once we find the suspect.

伊莎貝爾正和警方通報竊案。

警察：能否告訴我你的包包是什麼時候被偷的嗎？

伊莎貝爾：我認為小偷是中午我在喬伊斯咖啡館吃午餐時拿走它的。

警察：你有損失任何貴重物品嗎？

伊莎貝爾：我有 500 美元現金、一臺相機和護照在包包裡。

警察：好的，我們會調閱監視器。一旦我們找到嫌疑犯，就會聯絡你。

🎧 30-4

Justin is reporting the robbery to the police on the phone.

Officer: What is your emergency?

Justin: I was robbed!

Officer: Where did it happen?

Justin: It happened at Queen Avenue.

Officer: Can you describe your robber?

Justin: He is about 6 feet tall and has long brown hair. He's wearing a black T-shirt and blue jeans.

賈斯汀正在電話中和警方通報搶案。

警察：有什麼緊急狀況？

賈斯汀：我被搶了！

警察：在哪裡發生？

賈斯汀：在皇后大道上發生。

警察：你可以描述一下搶匪嗎？

賈斯汀：他大約六呎高，留著咖啡色長髮。他穿著黑色 T 恤和藍色牛仔褲。

還能這樣說

1. I have lost mine.

I found my camra missing. 我發現我的相機遺失了。

I got robbed on the platform. 我在月臺被搶了。

I had my wallet stolen by a pickpocket at the resraurat.

我的錢包在餐廳被扒手偷走了。

2. Could you tell me when your bag was stolen?

Where do you lose your passport? 你是在哪裡遺失護照的？

Did you notice anyone suspicious? 你有注意到任何可疑的人士嗎？

Do you have any information about the robber?

你有任何關於搶匪的訊息嗎？

現在才知道

旅遊安全守則 🔍

在國外自助旅行時，一定要留意自身安全，以免發生意外或危險。

以下技巧學起來，讓你安心旅遊：

1. 注意自己的行李：託運行李要上鎖、隨身行李則要拉好拉鍊；一定要看顧好行李，不讓行李離開視線。因為歹徒可能趁你不注意時偷走你的物品，也可能在你的行李裡放入毒品等違禁物品。切記不要好心幫他人攜帶行李，萬一有違禁物品那可就百口莫辯，到時可能會面臨刑罰、甚至死刑。

2. 保持低調、財不露白：出國遊玩，衣著乾淨整齊就行，要避免過於光鮮亮麗、穿金戴銀，以免引起歹徒注意，進而成為行竊或行搶的目標。

3. 妥善保管貴重物品或重要證件：貴重物品要分散放在不同口袋或包包裡，以免被偷或被搶時，一次損失全部。如果放在背包裡，要將背包背在胸前。如果留在飯店房間，最好鎖進保險箱。

4. 不宜夜晚在外遊蕩：盡量避免半夜在外走動。夜晚除了視線不佳，路上行人也比較少，萬一發生意外也求救無門。

5. 不要隨便接受陌生人邀約：在人生地不熟的地方，就算看似友善的當地人邀請參與活動，也還是要保持警戒心，有時對方可能不懷好意。例如：一些知名景點會有裝扮成卡通人物或當地特色服飾的人邀請你合照；此時如果答應了，在合照後，他們就會獅子大開口向你索取高額的「拍照費用」，到時你也只好花錢消災，不然他們可能會不讓你離開。

6. 扒手常見的伎倆：無故推擠你、假裝問路或問時間、佯裝好心跟你說衣服弄髒了、偽裝成抱著嬰兒的婦女、佯裝乞丐騷擾、聘雇孩童行竊等都是扒手慣用的手法。扒手會在降低你的戒心和轉移你的注意力後下手行竊。

 護照遺失了，怎麼辦？快上外交部領事事務局網站查詢如何補辦護照吧！

突發狀況篇

兌換外幣、
領取現金

字彙出外景

🎧 31-1

❶ change/exchange *vt.* 兌換 (錢)

❷ break *vt.* 換成 (小鈔)

❸ exchange rate *n.* [C] 匯率

❹ (foreign) currency

　n. [C][U] (外國) 貨幣

❺ foreign currency exchange counter

　n. [C] 外幣收兌處

❻ change *n.* [U] 零錢

❼ bill/note *n.* [C] 紙鈔

❽ yen *n.* [C] 日圓 (¥)

❾ pound *n.* [C] 英鎊 (£)

❿ euro *n.* [C] 歐元 (€)

⓫ single *n.* [C] (美金) 1 元紙鈔

⓬ denomination *n.* [C] (錢的) 面額

⓭ traveling companion *n.* [C] 旅行同伴

⓮ commission/service fee *n.* [C] 手續費

⓯ withdraw *v.* 領取，提取

🎧 31-2

Louis, a hotel guest, is changing money at the front desk.

Receptionist: Good morning, sir. May I help you?

Louis: Yes. I'd like to exchange my dollars for yen.

Receptionist: No problem, sir. Could you please fill in this form?

Louis: Sure. (*Filling in the form*) OK. Here you are.

Receptionist: Thank you. Just a moment, please. I'll calculate that for you. (*After a while*) At today's exchange rate, 200 US dollars can be exchanged for 21,687 Japanese yen. Here are your Japanese yen.

Louis: Thanks.

飯店房客路易正在櫃臺兌換錢。

接待員：早安，先生。有什麼是我可以幫你的嗎？

路易：有的。我想把美元換成日圓。

接待員：沒問題，先生。可以請你填寫這張表嗎？

路易：當然可以。(*填表*) 好了。給你。

接待員：謝謝。請稍等一下。我來為你計算一下。(*過了一會兒*) 按照今天的匯率，200 美元可以兌換 21,687 日圓。這是你的日圓。

路易：謝謝。

🎧 31-3

Gloria is changing money at a foreign currency exchange counter.

Gloria: Hi, can I change some euros into US dollars?

Clerk: Of course. How much do you want to change?

Gloria: One hundred euros. What's the exchange rate for US dollars today?

Clerk: We have the best exchange rate. One euro to 1.15 US dollars. So, that comes to $115. In what denomination would you like your change?

Gloria: I'd like five twenties, one ten, and five singles.

Clerk: No problem.

葛蘿莉亞正在外幣收兌處換錢。

葛蘿莉亞：嗨，我可以把一些歐元兌換成美元嗎？

店員：當然可以。你想要換多少錢？

葛蘿莉亞：100 歐元。今天兌換美元的匯率是多少？

店員：我們有最優惠的匯率。1 歐元兌換 1.15 美元。所以一共是 115 美元。你所兌換的美元想要什麼面額？

葛蘿莉亞：我想要五張 20 美元、 張 10 美元和五張 1 美元。

店員：沒問題。

🎧 **31-4**

Richard is chatting with Amber, his traveling companion.

Richard: Oh, I didn't organize well. I've spent most of my cash.

Amber: No way! It's just the second day of our trip.

Richard: I thought I could use my credit card, so I didn't prepare much cash.

Amber: Could you use your card to withdraw cash overseas? But the bank might take a commission.

Richard: The commission is no big deal. Let's find an ATM now.

理查正在和旅行同伴安柏聊天。

理查：喔，我沒籌畫好。我已經花掉我大部分的現金。

安柏：不會吧！這只是我們旅行的第二天。

理查：我想說我能用信用卡，所以我沒準備太多現金。

安柏：你能用你的卡在國外領現金嗎？雖然銀行可能會收手續費。

理查：手續費不是大問題。現在我們來找臺自動櫃員機。

還能這樣說

1. I'd like to exchange my dollars for yen.

> to change some US dollars into pounds 把一些美元換成英鎊
>
> to break this $100 bill 把這張 100 美元紙鈔換成小鈔
>
> to break this into small bills 把這個換成小鈔
>
> change for this bill 把這張紙鈔換成零錢

2. In what denomination would you like your change?

> How would you like it? 你想怎麼換？
>
> In what denominations? 要什麼面額的？
>
> Would you like that in large or small bills? 你想要大鈔還是小鈔？

現在才知道

換外幣？

☆ 外幣兌換的方法

1. 銀行臨櫃兌換：至銀行填寫申請表並排隊等候，可能需支付手續費。

2. 線上結匯流程：在線上購買外幣，轉帳後即完成結帳，結帳後當天或隔天就能去銀行或機場銀行提領外幣現金。最大好處是匯率優惠且不用手續費。

3. 外幣提款機提領：用一般的金融卡即可，金額是從臺幣帳戶直接扣款。不僅匯率優惠更多，且二十四小時皆能提領外幣。若為跨行提領則需收跨行手續費。

4. 外幣帳戶提領：外幣帳戶通常是用來定存或買賣賺匯差，也可從中領取外幣，但需收取匯差手續費。

☆ 這樣換外幣，最划算

1. 先在國內銀行換：在國內銀行兌換外幣的匯率通常會比在機場、國外的飯店和外幣兌換店還要優惠。

2. 搞懂「現金匯率」和「即期匯率」：現金匯率是買賣外幣「現鈔」的價錢；即期匯率則是一般外幣帳戶的交易，外幣會存在帳戶裡，而非直接拿到現鈔。通常即期匯率會比現金匯率優惠一點喔。

3. 找到好時機：如果很早就安排出國計畫，不妨觀察外幣匯率、關心時事新聞，若遇到划算的匯率，就可以先兌換存在外幣帳戶裡，等要出國時再去領取。

4. 平日優於週末，早上優於下午：如果在國外飯店或外幣兌換店兌換外幣，就要記得這個小訣竅。因為銀行週末沒有營業，飯店或外幣兌換店無法確認匯率，為了避免匯率下降的損失，便把兌換匯率調得差一點。以此類推，因為業者來不及把下午收到的外幣存入銀行，下午的匯率會調得比白天差一點。

5. 不要兌換過多外幣：衡量旅遊的狀況兌換適量現金。如果兌換過多用不完，回國後要換回臺幣時，不但要付手續費，也會產生匯差的損失，很不划算。

突發狀況篇

生病就醫

 字彙出外景

🎧 **32-1**

1. clinic *n.* [C] 診所
2. pharmacy/chemist's *n.* [C] 藥局，藥房
3. pharmacist *n.* [C] 藥劑師
4. prescribe *vt.* 開 (藥)
5. prescription *n.* [C] 處方；處方藥
6. symptom *n.* [C] 症狀
7. stomachache *n.* [C] 胃痛，肚子痛
8. (food) allergy *n.* [C] (食物) 過敏
9. allergic *adj.* 過敏的
10. cough *vi.* 咳 (嗽)；*n.* [C] 咳嗽

11. runny nose *n.* [C] 流鼻水
12. headache *n.* [C] 頭痛
13. sore *adj.* (發炎) 疼痛的
14. fever *n.* [C][U] 發燒
15. take sb's temperature *phr.* 幫…量體溫
16. get/have (the) flu *phr.* 得到流感
17. get/catch a cold *phr.* 感冒
18. medication *n.* [C][U] 藥物
19. pill *n.* [C] 藥片，藥丸
20. tablet *n.* [C] 藥錠

旅遊英文
這樣就GO

🎧 32-2

Flora goes to a local clinic to visit a doctor.

Doctor: How can I help you today?

Flora: I've got an itchy rash all over my arms and legs.

Doctor: Let me take a look. How long has it been like that?

Flora: Since last night.

Doctor: Have you eaten anything special?

Flora: I had seafood hot pot last night.

Doctor: I see. Do you have any other symptoms?

Flora: Yes, I have a slight stomachache.

Doctor: I think you have a food allergy. Don't worry. It's nothing serious. I will prescribe you some medicine.

芙蘿拉去當地的一間診所就醫。

醫生：今天我可以怎麼幫你？

芙蘿拉：我的手臂和腿上長滿了很癢的疹子。

醫生：讓我看看。這樣的情況有多久了？

芙蘿拉：從昨天晚上開始。

醫生：你有吃什麼特別的食物嗎？

芙蘿拉：我昨天晚上吃了海鮮火鍋。

醫生：了解。你還有任何其他症狀嗎？

芙蘿拉：有，我有一點肚子痛。

醫生：我認為你是食物過敏。別擔心。不嚴重。我會開些藥給你。

🎧 32-3

Francis sees a doctor about his sickness.

Doctor: What seems to be the problem?

Francis: I'm not feeling well.

Doctor: What are your symptoms?

Francis: (*Coughing*) I have a bad cough, a runny nose and a terrible headache. Besides, my throat is sore.

Doctor: Let me take your temperature. (*After a while*) You are running a fever. I think you've got the flu. I'll write you a prescription for flu medications. Are you allergic to any medication?

Francis: No, I don't think so.

Doctor: Get this prescription filled at the pharmacy. You should be feeling better soon once you take the medicine.

佛朗西斯去看醫生治病。

醫生：你怎麼了？

佛朗西斯：我覺得不太舒服。

醫生：你有什麼症狀？

佛朗西斯：(*咳嗽*) 我咳得很厲害、流鼻水而且頭很痛。此外，喉嚨也很痛。

醫生：我幫你量體溫。(*過了一會兒*) 你正在發燒。我認為你得了流感。我會幫你開流感藥的處方。你有對任何藥物過敏嗎？

佛朗西斯：沒有。我想是沒有的。

醫生：拿這張處方去藥局領取藥物。你吃了藥應該很快就會覺得好一點。

 32-4

Elizabeth is talking to a pharmacist at a chemist's.

Pharmacist: Hi, how may I help you?

Elizabeth: I need this prescription filled, please.

Pharmacist: Sure. (*After a while*) Your prescription is ready.

Elizabeth: Thanks. (*Checking the items*) When should I take them?

Pharmacist: The red pills should be taken four times a day, after each meal and at bedtime. The white tablets should be taken once a day, at bedtime. You can read the instructions on the bags.

伊莉莎白正在藥局和藥劑師談話。

藥劑師：嗨，有什麼可以幫到你的嗎？

伊莉莎白：我要按照這張處方領取藥物，麻煩你。

藥劑師：沒問題。(過一會兒) 你的處方藥好了。

伊莉莎白：謝謝。(核對品項) 我什麼時候要吃藥？

藥劑師：紅色藥丸一天吃四次，三餐飯後和睡前吃。白色藥錠一天吃一次，睡前吃。你可以閱讀藥袋上的說明。

還能這樣說

1. I've got an itchy rash all over my arms and legs.

> a cold 感冒
>
> a headache 頭痛
>
> a terrible stomachache 肚子非常痛
>
> a (high) fever/temperature 發 (高) 燒
>
> a pain in my foot/back/chest 腳／背／胸口疼痛
>
> a bad cough, a runny nose, and a sore throat 咳嗽、流鼻水和喉嚨痛

2. How long has it been like that?

> How long have you been sick? 你生病多久了？
>
> How long have you been like this? 你維持這樣的狀況多久了？
>
> How long have you been feeling like this? 這個感覺持續多久了？

現在才知道

出遊生病!? 🔍

☆ **國外就醫好貴,生病該怎麼辦?**

若在國外旅遊時不小心生病或受傷得就醫,就會發現醫療費用非常昂貴。旅遊期間就醫已經有夠掃興,如果這時還要支付高額的醫療費用,實在是徹底破壞出遊的心情。以下幾招讓你在國外能夠安心就醫,減輕經濟負擔。

1. 挑選適合的旅遊保險:一般最常見就是旅遊平安險,投保前可以仔細比較各家保險公司的保障項目,選擇最適合自己的保險。若在旅遊期間真的遇到意外狀況,也可以得到相對應的理賠金額。

> **!** 如果旅遊時間較長,也可以考慮購買旅遊當地的保險喔!

2. 申請健保補助:若在國外需要緊急就醫,返臺後也能申請健保補助喔。不過要注意,除了要準備相關的申請文件,也要在一定時間內申請。更多相關資訊可至衛生福利部中央健康保險署網站查詢!

☆ 藥局購藥須知

　　因為在外國就醫成本昂貴，因此除非遇到緊急狀況需要去醫院就醫外，在只有輕微症狀的情況下，大多數人會選擇去藥局購買成藥服用。除此之外，國外有些保健食品和成藥也相當出名，不少人出國旅遊時會順道購買。不過，在購買成藥時，要注意以下兩點：

1. 詢問用藥方式、副作用 (side effect)：服用藥物前，一定要弄清楚用藥方式，同時，也可以詢問藥物是否有副作用。例如：若有需要自駕旅遊，那就不適合購買有嗜睡副作用的藥物。另外，如果有對部分藥物過敏的話，購買藥物前，也要再三確認欲購買的藥物是否有導致過敏的成分。

2. 藥物入境的數量限制：口服維生素藥品、感冒藥、蚊蟲叮咬藥等，向來是國人出國時喜歡購買的藥品。但是，藥物並不是想要買多少就買多少，入境數量是有限制的！相關規定可至財政部關務署網站查詢。

附錄 1 旅外國人急難救助

外交部領事事務局網站提供許多旅外安全的相關資訊，出國前不妨至該網站瀏覽，絕對能讓你在國外臨危不亂。

請至外交部領事事務局網站搜尋相關資料後填寫灰底方框！

● 欲出訪之國家：

● 駐外館處專線：

● 駐外館處地址：

機場出境大廳有提供「中華民國駐外機構緊急聯絡資訊」供民眾免費索取。

旅外國人急難救助全球免付費專線：

非急難救助情況，請避免撥打此專線。

 你知道外交部領事事務局也有 LINE 官方帳號嗎！？
加入外交部領事事務局 LINE 好友 (ID: @boca.tw)，你就可以查詢「行前準備」、「旅遊警示」、「急難救助」、「（搜尋）駐外館處」等各項超級實用旅外資訊喔！

附錄 2

行李表

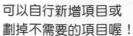
可以自行新增項目或劃掉不需要的項目喔！

重要證件／貨幣	搭機必備	清潔保養	衛生用品／藥品	3C 電器
☐ 護照	☐ 頸枕	☐ 牙膏／牙刷	☐ 面紙	☐ 手機
☐ 護照影本	☐ 口罩	☐ 卸妝乳	☐ 濕紙巾	☐ 手機充電器
☐ 備用護照照片 2 張	☐ 拖鞋	☐ 洗面乳	☐ 衛生棉	☐ 相機
☐ 簽證	☐ 牙刷	☐ 洗／潤髮乳	☐ 酒精	☐ 相機充電器
☐ 駕照 (影本)	☐ 薄外套	☐ 沐浴乳	☐ 隱形眼鏡	☐ 筆電
☐ 國際駕照 (影本)	☐ 保溫瓶	☐ 化妝棉	☐ 毛巾	☐ 筆電充電器
☐ 身分證	☐ 護唇膏	☐ 面膜	☐ 牙線	☐ 行動電源
☐ 身分證影本	☐ 護手霜	☐ 乳液	☐ 棉花棒	☐ 記憶卡
☐ 電子機票	☐ 保濕噴霧	☐ 乳霜	☐ 眼藥水	☐ 萬國轉接頭
☐ 訂房確認信	☐ 耳塞	☐ 身體乳	☐ 感冒藥	☐ 變壓器
☐ 旅遊行程表	☐	☐ 防曬乳	☐ 暈車藥	☐ 上網 SIM 卡
☐ 信用卡	☐	☐ 漱口水	☐ OK 繃	☐ Wi-Fi 分享器
☐ 外幣	☐	☐	☐ 蚊蟲叮咬藥膏	☐
☐	☐	☐	☐	☐
☐	☐	☐	☐	☐
☐	☐	☐	☐	☐
☐	☐	☐	☐	☐

衣物			其他	
☐ 貼身衣物	☐	☐	☐ 軟式購物袋	☐
☐ 外出衣物	☐	☐	☐ 雨具	☐
☐ 拖鞋／鞋子	☐	☐	☐	☐
☐ 襪子	☐	☐	☐	☐
☐ 帽子／圍巾	☐	☐	☐	☐
☐ 太陽眼鏡	☐	☐	☐	☐

打包行李時也要注意託運相關規定喔！

簡易記帳表

日期	項目	外幣／臺幣	日期	項目	外幣／臺幣

新多益
黃金互動16週：

基礎篇／進階篇 (二版)

李海碩、張秀帆、多益900團隊 編著

依難易度分為基礎篇與進階篇，教師可依學生程度選用。

- ★ 本書由ETS認證多益英語測驗專業發展工作坊講師李海碩、張秀帆編寫，及多益模擬試題編寫者Joseph E. Schier審訂。

- ★ 涵蓋2018年3月最新改制多益題型。每冊各8單元皆附電子朗讀音檔及一份多益全真模擬試題。

英文成語典故
Tell Me Why

李佳琪 編著

《英文成語典故Tell Me Why》來幫你記憶英文成語！

· 統整超過400個常見且實用的英文成語，以典故、
  由來的方式，介紹背後蘊含的歷史背景與文化，
  有趣又輕鬆，加強你對英文成語的印象。

· 成語按照字母A~Z排列，更在書末附上索引，方便
  尋找特定成語。

· 每三回附贈一回「單元測驗」，讓你閱讀過後可
  以即時檢驗。

學習英文成語從今以後不再是一件煩心事！

學習英文成語就像a piece of cake！

國家圖書館出版品預行編目資料

旅遊英文這樣就GO／三民英語編輯小組彙編.－－初
版二刷.－－臺北市: 三民，2023
面；　公分

ISBN 978-957-14-7062-7　(平裝)
1. 英語 2. 旅遊 3. 會話

805.188　　　　　　　　　　　　　　　109020646

旅遊英文這樣就 GO

彙　　　編	三民英語編輯小組
審　　　訂	許惠姍
發 行 人	劉振強
出 版 者	三民書局股份有限公司
地　　　址	臺北市復興北路 386 號 (復北門市)
	臺北市重慶南路一段 61 號 (重南門市)
電　　　話	(02)25006600
網　　　址	三民網路書店 https://www.sanmin.com.tw
出版日期	初版一刷 2021 年 3 月
	初版二刷 2023 年 11 月
書籍編號	S870800
I S B N	978-957-14-7062-7

三民書局